Jane
in
Bloom

Jane in Bloom

DEBORAH LYTTON

DUTTON CHILDREN'S BOOKS

DUTTON CHILDREN'S BOOKS
A division of Penguin Young Readers Group

Published by the Penguin Group • Penguin Group (USA) Inc., 375 Hudson Street, New York,
New York 10014, U.S.A. • Penguin Group (Canada), 90 Eglinton Avenue East, Suite 700, Toronto,
Ontario M4P 2Y3, Canada (a division of Pearson Penguin Canada Inc.) • Penguin Books Ltd,
80 Strand, London WC2R 0RL, England • Penguin Ireland, 25 St Stephen's Green, Dublin 2,
Ireland (a division of Penguin Books Ltd) • Penguin Group (Australia), 250 Camberwell Road,
Camberwell, Victoria 3124, Australia (a division of Pearson Australia Group Pty Ltd)
Penguin Books India Pvt Ltd, 11 Community Centre, Panchsheel Park, New Delhi–110 017, India
Penguin Group (NZ), 67 Apollo Drive, Rosedale, North Shore 0632, New Zealand (a division of
Pearson New Zealand Ltd.) • Penguin Books (South Africa) (Pty) Ltd, 24 Sturdee Avenue,
Rosebank, Johannesburg 2196, South Africa • Penguin Books Ltd, Registered Offices:
80 Strand, London WC2R 0RL, England

CIP Data is available.

Published in the United States by Dutton Children's Books,
a division of Penguin Young Readers Group
345 Hudson Street, New York, New York 10014
www.penguin.com/youngreaders

Designed by Elizabeth Frances

Printed in USA   First Edition

10 9 8 7 6 5 4 3 2 1   ISBN 978-0-525-42078-1

Young adult
FICTION

APR 0 6 2009

177937

For Ava and Caroline

Jane
in
Bloom

Chapter 1

I open my eyes.

And I realize. Today is the day. Today is my twelfth birthday.

Today I am finally old enough to get my ears pierced.

I jump out of my soft lavender bed and stand in front of the mirror barefoot in my blue pajamas with little white puffy clouds all over the legs. I turn this way and that way. To be truthful, I'm a little disappointed. I don't look older at all. I'm still the same me. The anomaly in an all-blond-haired, blue-eyed family with my red curly hair, army-green eyes, and a freckle for every day of my life—which would be somewhere around 4,380.

"Jane, breakfast!" my mother calls from downstairs.

"Coming," I call out.

"And get your sister," my mother adds.

Just then I notice something different, and I peer closer to be sure. There it is. A new freckle, right on the bridge of my nose. Number 4,381. Not exactly what I had in mind. But by tonight I will look different, I remind myself. By tonight, I will have pierced ears.

I turn toward the bathroom door. We have one of those bathrooms that connects my sister's room and my room, with a lilac-colored door on my side and a rose-colored door on Lizzie's side.

My door is locked from the inside, and I can hear water running.

"Lizzie," I call. "Breakfast."

I hear the toilet flush and then my sister's muffled voice, "No thanks."

I shrug and turn back toward the mirror. *"Happy Birthday,"* I tell myself with a smile.

When I get downstairs, I see a shiny pink-and-silver "Happy Birthday" banner hanging over the doorway to the dining room.

My father is already sitting at the table, reading the *New York Times*.

"Hi, Dad," I say as I make my way to his chair.

"Hi, honey," he responds. He breaks away from his reading long enough to say, "Happy Birthday." I drop a kiss on his cheek and then turn to look for my presents.

On the small, round table underneath the window, I see three wrapped boxes. One large rectangle and two smaller squares. I hold my breath. I've been hinting madly for a digital camera. Could it be? I resist the urge to shake the boxes. I'm twelve today, not five. I can wait.

I sit down at the table.

I might be able to control myself from shaking boxes, but there is something much more important on my mind this morning, and I can't hold it in.

I've noticed that if I tell my parents something as though I'm the parent, I get a better response, so I say it very matter-of-factly, "You and Mom said on my twelfth birthday— and that's tod—"

Just then my mother comes in from the kitchen, carrying a plate of banana-chocolate-chip pancakes, my absolute and total favorite.

"Mom! You remembered!" I exclaim, and jump up to hug her.

She smiles at me. "As though I haven't made this for you every birthday since you were three," she teases.

"True," I say. "But today is *extra* special."

"Twelve is a big birthday," my mother agrees. "Something is supposed to happen today, only I can't seem to remember what . . ." My mother is always pretending not to remember things that are really important to us. Like getting my ears pierced.

"Can we go after breakfast, *please?*" I beg, completely forgetting my parentlike voice.

"I think we said thirteen," my father says as he turns a page. I can't tell if he's teasing me or not.

"No, no, you said twelve! Believe me, I'm sure of it. I've been waiting seven whole years. Misty got them done in second grade; Zoe in *kindergarten*. I'm probably the only girl over ten in America—no, wait—*in the entire universe,* who doesn't have her ears pierced."

My mother places a heaping stack of pancakes in front of me. "I always said you had the memory of an elephant," she says. "If you're not busy after breakfast, I thought we might head over to the mall."

"I'm not busy," I say as I dive into the pancakes.

"Where's your sister?" my mother asks as she brushes her hand across her perfectly-combed-into-a-chignon, never-a-hair-out-of-place, blond head.

"I called her," I say with my mouth full of pancakes.

"She's not going to pull this again," my father says.

"Harold," my mother responds. "I went ten rounds yesterday over a glass of milk."

My father stands and throws his paper to the ground. "When is she going to stop this nonsense?" His mouth pinches into a tight, straight line.

My mother walks to the doorway. I watch her hands as they reach up to her already perfect hair and smooth it back.

"Elizabeth," she calls sweetly. "Breakfast is on the table."

Silence.

"I'll get her," I tell them. I pass under the "Happy Birthday" sign and head up the stairs.

Lizzie is my parents' perfect child. The one they are always bragging about to their friends. She's sixteen years old. Gorgeous. Popular. A straight-A student. Lizzie, with long, straight hair the color of sunshine, blue eyes the color of the sky on a summer day, and a smile full of cloud-white never-had-braces-but-are-still-perfect teeth. She doesn't have a freckle on her.

When Lizzie walks into a room, the air changes. It whirls around her, like an attention tornado. Everyone wants to be near her.

Knock. Knock.

"Lizzie?" I call out softly. No response.

I open the door a crack. The shutters are closed and the room is dark, but I can still see her. Lizzie, hunched over her desk. Writing. It occurs to me that my sister is always hunched over lately. I wonder why I never noticed it before.

In the shadows, I spot the photographs taped around the edges of Lizzie's mirror. There are models in bathing suits, actresses at film premieres, marathon runners, cheerleaders, homecoming queens. All of Lizzie's goals end up on the mirror. She calls it her Secret of Success.

I take a step into the room. Maybe she didn't hear me.

"Lizzie . . ." I try. I stop when I hear her words.

"Not hungry."

"That's not the point," I say, trying to be parentlike.

"Not hungry," she says again.

"Please . . . for me." *It's my birthday.* I don't say this part. I don't know why; I just don't.

Through the darkened room, I see her stand up. As she comes toward me, the light from the hallway shines on her. In the spotlight, Lizzie is all golden. And truly moviestar gorgeous. Except my sister looks like she's carrying the weight of the world on her shoulders.

She clutches a tiny turquoise box in her right hand.

All of a sudden tears burn my eyes and all I know is I want to hug her. I reach out my arms and wrap them around her. She feels so fragile. Like she might break if I squeeze her too hard. She leans into me for a second. And then she's gone. Back into that place she goes. Where I can't come.

She holds out the box to me. *"Happy Birthday, J,"* she whispers softly, liltingly, in her beautiful voice. She's called me J since I can remember.

"Thanks," I murmur as I touch my fingers to the box, suddenly self-conscious. I start to untie the little silver ribbon, but Lizzie stops me.

"Open it later," she tells me.

"Okay," I say as I gently take her hand and lead her down to the lion's den.

Back at the table, we all pretend everything is normal. Except that Lizzie hasn't eaten a bite of food. I, on the other hand, am on my second stack of pancakes.

And then it begins.

My mother looks at Lizzie, who is cutting a grape into four pieces.

"Honey, why don't you try a pancake?" My mother is like a food cheerleader.

"I hate pancakes." This is her new thing. She hates everything my mother wants her to eat.

"Nonsense." (My father's favorite word.) "Pass the toast, Elizabeth."

I take another bite of pancakes. Gulp orange juice.

"You used to love them." My mother won't give up.

"Well, I don't anymore."

"Be happy," my mother urges. "Smile."

My sister doesn't smile. And she doesn't reach for the large plate of toast either, so I do it for her. My dad is back inside the business section and doesn't even notice who has handed him the plate.

"Thank you, dear," he mumbles.

"I'm not eating the pancakes," Lizzie announces.

Now my father looks up from the paper. *Uh-oh*, I think. And I start shoveling food into my mouth.

"Doesn't matter, you're going to eat it, young lady."

It's amazing. I'm shaking in my chair, but Lizzie is totally unfazed.

"No," she says firmly.

My father looks at my mother. I think he must be really mad. We don't say no to him. Ever. My mouth is so full I have to breathe through my nose. I gulp some milk to wash the pancakes down.

And then he uses it. The Voice. He never yells, he doesn't have to. He just uses The Voice. It's low and grav-

elly, and sounds like a volcano rumbling down in the center of the earth, ready to erupt. "Enough of this nonsense.
I'll hear no more of it."

I want to be invisible. I wish I could close my eyes and
just disappear. Go someplace quiet. A beach somewhere, a
treetop, a cloud.

"Just eat five bites." My mother, the hostage negotiator.

Lizzie glares at her.

My father reaches for his coffee. Stirs ivory cream into
the java. I watch it swirl, wondering how he can be so
calm.

"Three?" My mother is backing down already.

Lizzie crosses her arms over her bony chest. Her mouth
in a thin line.

My mother moves to stand behind Lizzie's chair. I've
now moved on to sausage. I'm not even cutting it, just
stabbing the links with my fork and biting.

My mother cuts three smallish bites of pancake on
Lizzie's plate. She spears one and wedges the fork into
Lizzie's fist.

Lizzie's eyes meet mine. I can see the glisten of tears in
the pools of blue. She speaks to me without words. It's a
language I've been speaking since I was a baby. I understand
Lizzie's facial cues as though words were coming from her

lips. Her eyebrows raise slightly, her mouth crinkles. Lizzie is telling me she's sorry this is happening right now. She hasn't forgotten it's my day. But she can't help it.

I give her a look back. It's a look I've been giving her my whole life, and with twelve years of practice, I'm really good at it. I tilt my head to the left and give a small half smile without teeth. This is the look that says, *It's okay. Don't worry about it.* I don't really feel this. What I really feel is that everyone should just smile and eat breakfast together. Because a girl's birthday is the one day of the year that should be about her. Instead, I take care of Lizzie. She's counting on me.

Lizzie gives me back a look with a small relieved smile. More tears in the pools. And this is her way of thanking me.

While my sister and I are wordlessly conversing, Mom is waiting. Her arms are crossed over her chest and she is waiting on Lizzie to eat. Dad is waiting, his eyes fixed on Lizzie's plate.

Lizzie stabs one teeny piece of pancake and lifts it to her mouth. Ever so slowly. She opens her mouth, still watching me. And slips the morsel between her lips. Then she chews. And chews. And chews. She must chew fifty times. I can hear her jaw grinding. There can't possibly be any food left between her teeth. But still she keeps on grinding.

I can't watch. I look down at my plate and count the flowers along the edge of the china. One rose, two daisies, three pansies, four—

"There," she announces triumphantly as she plunks the fork back onto the plate.

"It's a start," my mother admits encouragingly. But that's it. Lizzie has eaten all she's going to eat for the morning.

"May I be excused?" Lizzie asks softly.

"Go ahead," my father answers.

"I'm going for a run," Lizzie announces. And before I know it, she's out the door.

My mother makes a soft sound like a kitten mewing. I recognize it as her version of a sob. But we don't cry in the Holden family. At least not in front of anybody.

Within seconds, she escapes to the kitchen. And out the back door. Probably for a cigarette. She thinks we don't know that she smokes. She promised us she would quit over two years ago, but the smell of smoke is a dead give-away. (The mints she eats and the gardenia perfume she sprays on do nothing to cover the smell of Virginia Slims.) And anyway, who spends that much time in the garage?

After a minute, my father stands and leaves the table.

And I sit there, too stuffed to move, and stare at the sparkly pink sign.

Chapter 2

For ten minutes, I sit at the empty table. Then I pry myself
out of the chair, and go outside to find Lizzie. I know her
route, but I can't begin to run on such a full stomach. I
walk down the street instead. It gives me time to think.
About other birthdays. I remember my fourth birthday.
My parents gave me a set of crayons and special art paper. I
tried to draw a flower, but it kept coming out all lopsided.
I remember crying. Until Lizzie sat behind me on the floor,
placed her hand around mine, and drew the flower with
me. And then we drew another. And another. Until the en-

tire paper was a garden of the most beautiful flowers I had ever seen. Then she helped me color them. We made pink roses, red geraniums, purple irises, yellow daffodils, blue cornflowers, orange poppies. I was so proud of that picture. Lizzie refused to take any credit for it, boasting to my parents that I had drawn it all by myself. It was our secret.

I see Lizzie running toward me now, her blond hair flowing behind her like a yellow scarf blowing in the wind. When she sees me, she slows down.

"Don't you ever get sick of pretending to be happy all the time?" She pants as she speaks.

I shrug. I don't really know what to say. "I guess."

"What do you think would happen if I brought home a C?" Lizzie asks, her blue eyes sparkling with the thought.

"Would you?" I ask. I can't even imagine such a thing. Lizzie has always been a straight-A student.

She shrugs. "Maybe." She bends over to touch the ground, stretching her legs.

"I could give you pointers," I tell her. "I bring home C's all the time."

Lizzie throws back her head and laughs at this. I love her laugh. It sounds like little tiny crystal bells. I smile big and slip my hand into hers. And that's how we walk all the way home.

As soon as we get back to the house, I go to find my mother. I am only thinking of one thing. Getting my ears pierced. I find her sitting in her favorite green-and-white-checked armchair. Staring at the wall. Whenever she sits here, she's upset about something.

"Mom," I say softly. "Can we go to the mall now?"

"In a little bit," she answers without looking at me.

Hours later, I'm painting my fingernails purple when the phone rings. "How do they look?" my best friend Zoe asks. She's wondering about my pierced ears. Only I haven't gotten them yet. It's two-thirty and my earlobes are still untouched. Mom's still sitting in the checked chair. It's like she's forgotten I even exist.

"I didn't get them yet," I tell her.

"Why not?" She asks.

"My mom had some papers to grade. She promised we'll go as soon as she's done," I lie. I don't know why I do it. Zoe is my best friend in the whole world and we tell each other everything. But for some reason, I don't feel like talking about it. Zoe's one wish is to have a big sister. Sometimes she even pretends that Lizzie is her sister, too. I can't tell her that Lizzie isn't perfect. It would ruin her dream.

Zoe is rambling on and I haven't even heard a word she's been saying.

"Hello, Earth to Jane! I *asked* if you want me to come over and hang out for a while. Do you?" Zoe offers.

"I better not. I mean, my mom is going to be ready soon, and I think she wanted this to be something special for the two of us." I'm getting too good at this lying thing.

"Anyway, I'll see you at six, right?" She's asking about tonight. Tonight. My mom was going to take Zoe and Lizzie and me out to dinner and a movie. I was so excited before. Now I don't know what to think.

"Yeah," I mumble.

"Jane, you okay?" Zoe asks, her voice gentle. "You sound kind of depressed."

"I guess I'm a little bit tired," I lie again. "I didn't really sleep last night. I was so excited about today."

"Me, too." I can practically hear her smiling into the phone.

"I'm borrowing my mom's black leather jacket and silver hoop earrings." Silver hoops. I feel the tears start to burn behind my eyes and I blink them back. No way. I'm not crying over this. I'm still the Birthday Girl, I tell myself. And the day's barely half over.

Hours later, Mom is supposed to be getting ready to go. I'm sitting at my dressing table, coaxing my unruly locks into tiny braids with beads at the bottom. It's five-thirty and no one has talked to me for hours.

Lizzie's been in her room in the dark, hunched over the desk, scribbling madly into one of her journals. Mom is in some kind of trancelike state. Dad mumbled something about work and escaped to the office hours ago. I think I should have taken Zoe up on her offer. But I'm not in the mood to be with anyone anymore.

I look at my unpierced ears and try to think of something positive. I draw a blank.

Then there's a knock on my door.

"Jane, may I come in?" Dad asks.

I have one of those cliché "Keep Out" signs on my door, only I've decorated it with purple butterflies and blue hearts. No one takes it seriously except my dad. Because he has absolutely no sense of humor. He can't see the irony in a cheerful "Keep Out" sign.

"Yeah," I call out to him.

I know as soon as I look at his face. But I wait for him to tell me.

"Your mother isn't up to going tonight."

Okay, I think. *So that's it.*

But what he says next surprises me.

"So I thought, if it's okay with you and Zoe, I'll take you."

My dad. Taking us to dinner and a tween movie. It's too funny for words. But I don't laugh because I know that's the last thing on earth he'd want to do. And that he's doing this for me. I smile at him.

"Do you have something to wear?" I tease.

"Is it special attire?" he asks, straight-faced. My dad gets nothing.

"Ties aren't allowed," I tell him.

"Maybe you can pick something out for me," he offers. I smile and head for his closet. I'm rifling through my dad's few items of casual clothing, trying desperately to pull together something remotely decent, when I hear my mother's voice. She's yelling at Lizzie to open the bathroom door.

I step out into the hallway, bright under the yellow eighty-watt bulbs. I can hear muffled sounds coming from Lizzie's bedroom. I head for my room. Lizzie's room is closer, but I don't want to experience a repeat of breakfast. I tiptoe into my room. That's when I hear Lizzie coughing. I feel a sick sinking in the pit of my stomach as I head for the bathroom door. I pull my braids out of the way so that I can press my ear against the cool lavender door and listen. The water is running. I hear her cough again, and then the toilet flushes.

I knock twice on the door. It's our signal. "Lizzie," I call out.

Nothing.

I try the handle. Locked. She turns off the water.

I lean my forehead against the door and take a deep breath, the kind I've been practicing in yoga. Zoe's mom is a yoga teacher and she lets us take her classes sometimes. I like the meditation part when she plays this soft music with running water in the background. We lie on the floor with our eyes closed and focus on the spot right between our eyebrows. It's kind of like praying, but different. Whenever I pray, I always end up asking for things, even if I try not to. When I meditate, I just let myself *be*. I've noticed that when I do the yoga breathing even outside of class, it helps me to relax.

I close my eyes and drift into the space between my eyes. I focus on the white spot of light there. *Breathe,* I tell myself. It's always about Lizzie. Always has been. Today was supposed to be about me. *Breathe. Breathe. Breathe.*

When I speak, my voice is so soft, I don't think she will even hear it.

"You're my best friend, Lizzie—please don't shut me out. I love you."

She must hear me, because she unlocks the door. I wait a few seconds and then slide it open. I close the door behind me and lock it again.

Lizzie is curled up on the floor. Right in the center of the pink flower Pottery Barn carpet. Her frail arms are wrapped tightly around her knees and her eyes are swollen from crying.

She doesn't look at me. Her voice is a hoarse whisper.

"No one should love me."

Pain shoots through my heart. I forget all about my birthday, all I want to do is make her feel better.

"Oh, Lizzie," I say as I kneel beside her and reach out for her arm. But she shrinks away before I can touch her.

"Don't," she snarls.

I lean back on my heels and watch her. I don't know how to help my sister.

"I already gained a pound," she confides. "Imagine if I would have eaten all they wanted, I'd have gained twenty."

"You didn't even eat anything." I try to think of something she likes. Then I come up with it.

"What about cake? It's your favorite—chocolate."

Lizzie covers her ears.

"You don't understand!" she yells at me. "Leave me alone. You're one of them!"

"No, I'm not!" I yell back.

But she keeps chanting, "You're one of them, you're one of them."

"No, I'm not! Stop it. I'm not one of them. Quit saying that!" She keeps yelling at me with her hands over her ears. I want her to stop it. It's not my fault. She's screaming at me. The same words over and over. I tell her to stop it, but she won't. I throw open the bathroom door and run into Lizzie's room.

"What in the world! Jane!" I hear my mother's voice like I am underwater. It sounds muffled and far away.

"What's wrong with everybody around here!" I am screaming. But I don't care because I have lost control.

My father has appeared in the doorway. His eyes meet mine, and for an instant I wonder if I have gone too far. He looks really mad. I feel my stomach tighten up.

"Go to your room, Jane," he says in The Voice.

I do. And I stay there for the next half hour. I lie on my bed and plot my future. I imagine packing up all my things and leaving.

I have just remembered that I should call Zoe—make up some more lies to tell my best friend—when I hear a scream coming from Lizzie's room. It's my mother. She's shrieking.

I run toward the bathroom and fling open the door, making it there before my dad. I barely notice my mother, who is holding Lizzie's head in her lap.

"She's unconscious. Call an ambulance," she yells to my father. I can't move.

I am standing in the center of Lizzie's bedroom when the paramedics arrive. Two men hurry into the bathroom, led by my father. One of them carries medical supplies and the other, a stretcher.

"She's been dieting quite a bit," my mother is explaining. I watch as they lean over my sister, who is awake now and looks terrified. Lizzie's eyes meet mine, and I see her silent plea for help. I try to tilt my head to the left and give the small half smile without teeth that I know she's looking for. I don't know if I succeed because she closes her eyes.

I feel like someone is choking me. I start to pant. Gasping for air. Then I feel my father's hands heavy like weights on my shoulders. He steers me into the hallway.

Breathe, I tell myself. *Breathe.* I close my eyes and focus on the light I see there. *Breathe in peace, breathe out fear. Breathe in peace, breathe out fear.*

I open my eyes to see the paramedics carry my Lizzie past me. Her eyes are still closed. For a split second, I think she's dead. I open my mouth to speak, but nothing comes out. I swallow and try again.

"Is she going to be okay?" I wonder if anyone has understood me, because I suck the words into my throat as I say them. But the blond paramedic must hear my voice because he looks up at me.

"We gave her something to help her rest right now. We're going to take good care of her, don't you worry."

My mother takes my hand as we follow the stretcher down the stairs. But I pull it away and stick it in my pocket instead. She doesn't say anything, and I'm glad. I feel sick to my stomach. All I can think about is Lizzie. And how this is all my fault. I fought with her. And then I left her alone when she needed me. I look down at my feet as they walk down the stairs one by one. Just this morning, Lizzie and I were walking down the stairs together to have my birthday breakfast.

The doors to the ambulance are open. The paramedics are about to put Lizzie into the back. My mother climbs in and waits. There is an oxygen mask over Lizzie's mouth and nose. Her face looks so tiny and pale underneath the plastic. Her eyes are still closed. The sight of it makes my eyes start to blur. I reach out and lightly stroke her silky hair back from her face.

"Excuse me," the nice paramedic says to me. "We have to go now." I nod slowly. I can't speak. They lift the stretcher into the ambulance. I see my mother looking at me as they close the doors, but I can tell she doesn't see me.

The siren screams into the night. It sounds like *Lizzie. Lizzie. Lizzie.*

I am frozen in place. Watching as the ambulance disappears into the night. My father suddenly appears next to me, gesturing toward his navy Volvo.

"Let's go, Jane." I nod. Nodding seems to be my only way of communicating at the moment. I climb into the passenger seat and buckle up. I sit silently and look out the window.

My mind is numb. I look—but see nothing.

Until we pass by the mall. And then I remember.

Zoe. The movie. My birthday.

"Dad, can I use your phone?" I ask. "I have to call Zoe."

He nods and hands me the phone without a word.

I dial Zoe's number. She answers on the first ring.

"Jane. What's going on? You guys are so late. We're going to miss the previews and everything!"

I reach for something to say. I end up somewhere between the truth and a half-truth.

"It's Lizzie. She's—she's sick," I stumble over the words.

"Oh my God. Is she okay?" Perfect Lizzie. Zoe's dream sister. Lying in the back of an ambulance.

"Yeah. She's going to be okay. But we're taking her to the emergency room just in case."

"What is it? Food poisoning or something?"

"I guess." Yeah. Food poisoning. Food poisoning the mind.

Zoe is silent for a while. Then she speaks.

"So, I guess we're not going, then." There is disappointment in her voice. I know she doesn't want me to know. After all, I just told her that Lizzie's sick. But she's disappointed. And the truth is, so am I.

I sigh. "No, I guess not."

"I'm sorry, Jane," she says softly. She knew how much this night meant to me. I shrug, even though she can't see. I'm used to pretending things don't matter to me when they really do.

"'S okay."

"You want me to come to the hospital with you? My mom could drive me."

I want this more than anything in the world. But instead I say no.

"Call me in the morning," Zoe tells me before she hangs up.

I hand the phone back to my father. And the rest of the ride is silent.

Chapter 3

The hospital is loud and filled with that bright fluorescent light that makes you squint and gives you an instant headache. Lizzie has already been taken into emergency. We all sit side by side on a blue tweed sofa.

I can't stop thinking about how this is all my fault. If I were my parents, I would hate me for doing this to Lizzie. So I am not prepared for my mother to reach out and take my hand. This time I let her.

"She's going to be okay, Jane. Don't worry."

She doesn't look at me when she speaks, and her voice

sounds almost mechanical. But I know she is trying to comfort me. Even if her words sound hollow.

I could really use a hug. But something stops me from asking my mother for one, or from just reaching out to her. Instead, I settle for her lightly stroking my hand.

Time moves so slowly as we sit there that I am certain it has stopped altogether. I am convinced that any second, someone is going to come out of the operating room and tell us that they have done all they could, but she's dead. Like they do on all those medical TV shows. So when a young doctor comes to tell us we can see Lizzie, I'm completely shocked.

We all stand and follow her into a room where Lizzie is hidden by a blue curtain. The doctor pulls it aside and there is my sister. In a mint-green hospital gown. With tubes coming out of her mouth. She looks like someone else. Not like Lizzie.

We don't stay long. Lizzie is barely awake and the doctor says we should all go home and rest. I kiss her softly on the cheek and whisper in her ear.

"I love you, Lizzie."

The drive home is quiet. No one says a word. Dad unlocks the front door and we file in and head our separate ways.

I look around the living room. I feel like a stranger in my own house. All I notice is the silence. The pink sparkly "Happy Birthday" banner waves in the doorway to the dining room. The wrapped presents sit on the side table, still waiting to be opened. They belonged to the Birthday Girl. I'm not her anymore. Then I notice my birthday cake. Someone has eaten half of it.

That's when I understand. Lizzie ate the chocolate cake. That's why she was so upset. Without even thinking, I pick up the cake and carry it to the kitchen. I shove the cake into the trash. I hide the evidence of Lizzie's sickness. I keep Lizzie's secret.

I am still standing over the trash can looking at the mushed cake when I finally taste the first tears on my lips.

Mom and Dad have already gone to bed by the time I creep up the stairs. I lower my head as I pass Lizzie's room. I breathe a sigh of relief when I walk through my own door and head for the comfort of my bed. Sinking into my purple butterfly comforter, I can't help but notice the open bathroom door. I tiptoe over and quickly shut the door without looking inside. I may never be able to go in there again.

I fall back into bed. Then I see it. The turquoise box.

Lizzie's gift to me. I almost forgot. I never opened it. I pick it up and hug it to my chest.

"Oh, Lizzie," I cry out. "I'm so sorry." I gently untie the ribbon and peel back the shiny blue paper.

Silver hoops.

It is 8 A.M. Sunday morning. I'm sitting in the kitchen, dressed and ready to go see Lizzie. I have been ready since six. I couldn't go back into the bathroom, so I showered downstairs. I smell sort of perfumey, from using the shampoo and soap in the guest bathroom. Not like my usual coconut Body Shop shampoo. It makes me feel like I'm not myself. Which I'm not, really.

My parents are in crisis mode. Which for them means not speaking. About anything. The house is still, even though I know that both of them are up.

I hope that Mom didn't notice my birthday cake in the trash. I feel bad now about throwing it away. I know she spent all night Friday making it for me. I tell myself that I am going to be really good today and not say anything to cause any trouble. I won't even speak.

I don't feel like eating anything. The thought of food actually makes me feel sick. But I pour myself a glass of milk because I don't have anything else to do. I'm tracing

Lizzie's name on the glass when my mom clips into the kitchen. She's dressed in church clothes. A pink suit with a white silk blouse. And heels. We're going to the hospital. She's clearly in denial.

She speaks without looking at me. "Jane, I'm going to get the car ready. Go and see if your father is ready, will you?"

She needs a smoke. *Why can't she just say it?* I wonder. But I go along with her charade. I always do.

"Sure," I say quietly. I hop off the chair and head for the stairs.

My dad is tying his tie. A tie? *Who are these people? And how can I possibly be related to them?*

"Aren't you guys a little overdressed?" I ask. I'm trying to make a joke, anything to break the silence.

"You don't think I should wear a tie?" he asks me. When he turns toward me, I feel like someone just poured ice cold water over my heart. I've never seen my dad look like this. His eyes are all red and swollen from crying and his skin is so white that his lips look blue. It scares me.

"No, it's fine," I murmur. *Get me out of here!* my mind screams.

The car ride is torture. My mother reeks of smoke and the perfume she sprayed on to cover it up. My father has put on way too much cologne. Between the two of them, I'm suffocating. I roll down the window and gulp for air.

"Jane, you're letting all the cold air out," my mother chides. I roll up the window. My last hope for escape.

The area where Lizzie is staying is "just for teenagers." I heard my mother tell my father she was glad of that, at least. But I'm not so sure there's *anything* to be glad about when we step off the elevator. All I can hear is screaming. Horror-movie kind of screaming. And someone laughing, like a hyena. It's freezing cold up here and I wish I had worn my ski jacket, or a heavy sweatshirt at least.

Lizzie is in 1208. It's at the end of a mint green hall. I notice locked gates everywhere. Like we're in prison or something. It makes me want to stand closer to my dad. So I do. When we find 1208, the door is closed. I feel sick to my stomach. Lizzie had to sleep here last night. Alone. I can't wait to see her and make sure she's okay.

But when the nurse leads us into Lizzie's room, I suddenly wish I had stayed home. She's lying in a stiff white bed, and her face looks as white as a blank sheet of paper. Her eyes are all red around the edges, and she's just staring. At nothing. The TV's not on. There's nothing on the walls, except for one of those wipe-off boards; it reads NURSE LACEY. There's a tube coming out of Lizzie's right arm. It connects to a clear bag of fluid. Looking at it gives me shivers up the back of my neck.

My mother sits down by Lizzie's side and talks to her softly. My father leans up against the window and stares out at the people walking on the sidewalk. I just stand in the middle of the room, feeling like an alien. I don't know where to look, what to say, what to do. It smells strange in here. Like cleaning solutions and old gym shoes. Lizzie's mouth is open, but no sound is coming out. I notice some drool forming on the side of her lips. I know she would hate this, if she had any idea what was going on, so I creep closer to wipe it off. That's when I notice the handcuffs. Well, not really handcuffs, but there are leather straps holding Lizzie's wrists to the bed.

I can't breathe. I'm going to throw up. I reach out for the door and I can't find it. I am grasping at something, pulling. I hear a dull shrieking, but I don't know where it's coming from. It sounds like a balloon losing its helium. Finally the door gives and I collapse into the hallway. The shrieking continues to follow me all the way to the front door. It is only when I reach the street that I realize I'm the one shrieking.

I sit on the curb until my parents pick me up. I have no idea how long I've been there. I don't even know what I've been thinking about. Just bits and pieces of Lizzie. I climb into the backseat and hunker down. No one speaks on the way home.

The rest of Sunday passes in a haze. We eat in shifts so no one has to speak. Zoe calls a few times, but I pretend to be busy. I can't talk. I try to concentrate on my Spanish homework. *Mi hermana esta bonita. Mi hermana esta delgada. My hermana . . .*

I don't know how to say "my sister is in the hospital, tied to a bed" in Spanish. But I think it would sound better than it does in English.

Chapter 4

Monday morning. I have to go to school today. I'm never allowed to skip school. I have had a perfect attendance record since the first grade. Even if I were dying, my parents wouldn't let me miss until I was actually dead. I think they don't let me miss school because then someone would have to stay home with me all day. So even today, with Lizzie in the hospital, hooked up to tubes, they make me go.

While Mom is downstairs making breakfast, I sneak into her closet and pull out a small red wood jewelry box. It's full of costume jewelry. I rummage through until I find what I'm looking for. Gold hoop clip-ons. I pinch one onto each ear, pull my hair forward to cover then, and I'm ready to go.

Then I hurry downstairs. Mom's cooking up eggs and turkey bacon, toast and smoothies. Dad's buried behind the paper. The only difference is that Lizzie's place is empty. *How can they just act like this?* I think. I want to scream, to break something. To make them notice. I still can't eat, so I push the food around on my plate. No one pays any attention.

Zoe's mom honks outside at ten to eight. Thank God today is her day for car pool.

I grab my backpack and my cleats. "See ya," I call out to no one in particular. I slam the back door and head down the driveway.

Zoe opens the back door, and I climb into her mom's minivan, careful not to step on any of the toys, sippy cups, and magazines covering the floor.

"Hi, Dee and Dum." I greet Zoe's twin brothers, who are strapped into their car seats. "Hi, Jane," they call out in unison. Their real names are Landon and Luke, but Zoe and I have dubbed them Tweedledee and Tweedledum.

Zoe smiles at me. Her golden eyes sparkle against her chocolate skin. I feel better already, just seeing her face.

"You definitely look older," she compliments.

"Thanks." I shrug.

"How's Lizzie?" she asks.

"She's okay," I mumble. I don't want to talk about Lizzie because then I'll have to lie to my best friend some more. There isn't a worse feeling than that.

"I'm glad," she says. Then Zoe holds out a small purple velvet box.

Normally, I'd rip into it immediately, but today I want to savor it.

"Open it," Zoe orders. I slowly lift the top of the box and find a black choker with a star pendant. The star is silver, but open so you can see through the middle. I love it. I tell her so as I put it around my neck.

"I almost forgot!" Zoe exclaims, and pulls my hair away from my left ear. When she sees, she lets my hair softly drop back to its place. She studies me with her warm eyes.

I look down at my fingers and pretend to see a hangnail. I know she can tell they're clip-ons, but she doesn't say anything.

"Did you get the camera?" she asks.

The camera. I don't even know. My presents are still sitting on the table, unopened. I smile with embarrassment and say nothing. Zoe takes my silence as a yes.

"That's perfect," she says. "Now you can take pictures at my tennis match Friday."

Great. I don't even know what's in that box.

Just then, Zoe's mom turns up the radio. "Oh, I love this song," she squeals. Zoe's mom starts singing really loud, and Zoe joins in. I turn and stare out the window, and conjugate the verb *estar*.

And then we're there.

I manage to make it through my Spanish quiz, fractions in math, and reading poetry aloud in English.

But that's all before lunch. Zoe and I sit under a big elm tree with our third musketeer, Misty.

I'm letting them do all the talking. Or Zoe mainly. She's chattering on about something she watched on television last night. I'm just thinking about Lizzie in that cold hospital room. Her hands tied down to the bed.

Just then, Kirsten Mueller walks up to us with her two minions, Emily and Gabrielle, and says, "Okay, Holden, let's see 'em."

I wasn't exaggerating when I told my parents that I'm pretty much the only sixth grader without pierced ears. And the worst part about it is, everyone knows. Including Kirsten, the snobbiest, most popular, and meanest girl in school.

I have totally forgotten about them. My earrings. Misty hasn't asked about them, probably because Zoe already told her about the clip-ons. But before I can say anything, Kirsten yanks my hair back and looks at my hoops. For a second, I think she's fooled, because she doesn't say anything. Then she starts laughing. Cackling, actually.

"Who'd you borrow those from, your grandmother?" she snarls as she yanks one hoop from my ear. "What a joke," she says as she tosses it on the ground. Emily and Gabrielle start snickering. Then she and the gruesome twosome walk off together. All I can think about is that I don't want to cry. I can feel Zoe and Misty staring at me. Zoe picks up the earring and hands it to me. I snap the other one off my ear and stuff both of them into my pocket. I can tell Zoe and Misty are looking at each other, trying to figure out what to say. But all I can do is try to think of something to make me not cry. I think of horses. Running across a field. A white one and a black one.

I bite into my sandwich. I can't taste it. We all pretend nothing has happened. But by the time we stand up, everyone in school knows about my fake earrings. Even the most popular boy in school, Hunter Baxley. I know because he stares at me as I walk past.

I keep moving, with Zoe on one side and Misty on the

other. I try not to notice all the kids pointing at me and laughing. I wonder if anyone has ever made fun of Kirsten. Probably not.

I go through the motions at soccer practice. It feels good to not to have to think for a little while. But right before it's time to go home, I have this overwhelming urge to run away. I wait until everyone else heads for the locker room and then I hurry to the bleachers. It's that or cry out in the open. I step out of the blinding sunlight into the blanket of shade underneath the bleachers just in time. The tears start falling so fast, I can't do anything to stop them. All I can do is let them out. I flop down in the soft grass, my hands covering my face.

"You okay?" I freeze. Someone has found me. I peek out from underneath my left hand to assess the intruder. Friend or foe? And it's the worst situation I could possibly imagine: Hunter Baxley. And he's close enough to see the tears on my cheeks. I wipe them away with the back of my hand even as I feel my chin jut out in defiance.

"Fine," I respond defensively. Being discovered makes me feel bristly all over, like a porcupine who wants to be left alone. The heat of humiliation sears through my face, and I close my eyes, willing myself to disappear.

When I open my eyes again, he's gone. And I can't be sure if I really saw him there at all. Or if I imagined him.

A few minutes later, I am climbing into my mother's white SUV. All traces of tears have been wiped from my cheeks.

"Hi, how was your day?" she asks, the same as she does every day. It's not a question that can be answered with anything but "Okay" or "Good" or "Fine, I got an A on my Spanish quiz." My mom doesn't really want to know how my day was, only that it was fine. How does she think it was? How could it possibly have been, with my sister in the mental ward?

I want to tell her that it was awful, that people laughed at me for pretending to have pierced ears, which I wouldn't have had to do if she'd taken me to get them pierced like she promised. Instead, I say, "Fine. It was fine."

At dinner, no one talks about Lizzie. We just pass the potatoes around. Dad asks me about school, and I mumble a generic reply. After days of not eating, I'm starved. Mom offers me more turkey. Then she busies herself clearing the table.

Sometimes you don't notice when everyone around you has gone mad. It happens so gradually that it just seems normal to you. And then, one day, you realize that nothing is the same anymore. It's like you are somewhere else, only with all the same people. And then it occurs to you that maybe the one who is different is you.

"Jane, you never opened your gifts," Mom says. As though I just forgot. The reason I never opened my gifts is unsaid. But we are all thinking about it.

So I just say a quiet, "I know."

Dad makes an effort. "Why don't you open them now?"

I shrug. I really don't want to. But now they both seem so focused on me. Maybe this is what Lizzie feels like all the time. Like a bug under glass.

My mother hands me the smallest of the boxes. I carefully pull back the pink paper. And there is the coveted digital camera. Only it doesn't matter to me so much anymore. I force a smile and thank my parents. The other boxes hold a carrying case and special photo paper.

It's really an incredible gift. And two days ago, I would have been jumping up and down with excitement. Instead, I get up and give both of them hugs.

"You're always using my camera. And I was twelve when my father gave me my first camera," Dad explains. "Though it wasn't digital in those days. Want me to help you set it up?"

"Maybe later," I offer. I just can't fake it anymore. I see something in his expression. I can't tell if it's disappointment or relief.

I mumble something about homework and escape to my room. I turn off the light and climb into bed fully clothed. I hide way down deep underneath the covers. Then I pull my knees up to my chin and bury my face there, wrapping my arms around my head like a hood. I am a teeny tiny ball of anguish. I weep silently. I feel the sobs shake my body so much that if my own arms weren't holding on, I think I would come apart.

Chapter 5

My favorite flowers are daisies. They're happy flowers. Simple flowers. Nothing ever goes wrong for a daisy.

Now, a rose is another story. A rose is very complicated. It's always changing on you. First it's a bud, and you think how pretty it looks. Then it starts to open and you're amazed because it's even more beautiful than before. When it opens all the way, it's so breathtaking that you have to touch it . . . and you do, but you forget about the thorns.

Lizzie is a rose. She's so beautiful and fragile that you have to reach out to her. You forget about the thorns.

She doesn't want pity. Which I understand. I wouldn't either. I would hate people feeling sorry for me, I think. On the day Lizzie comes home from the hospital, I try to cheer her up. I think she might like to listen to some music. But she won't even look at me. She just sits huddled in her bed, facing the wall. Then I ask her if she wants to come to the den and watch movies with me. She ignores me again.

The last time I went in there with one of her favorite magazines. I offered to cut out some photos for her. She threw the magazine on the floor. I've been sitting in a corner of the couch since then. I am hiding under the big pillow that normally sits on the back of the couch. It covers my body. I hope that no one will ever find me. But my dad does. I hear him come in and sit down on the other side of the couch. I know it's him because of his cologne. I love that I always know when my dad comes home because I can smell his cologne. I think maybe no one else in the world wears this kind because I've never smelled it on anyone except him.

I hear the rustle of his files. The scratch of his pen. It is oddly comforting.

Then, "Hi," he says quietly, without moving the pillows.

"Hi," I whisper back.

"Almost sat on you," he says.

I don't say anything back.

"Everything's going to be just fine," he tells me, but it sounds like he's really telling himself.

"I want her to be okay," I mumble.

"I know, honey," he says. "We all do."

It feels strange talking to him like this. I barely remember this dad. It's like the whole world is turned upside down. Lizzie is a stranger and Dad is sharing his feelings. Well, sort of, anyway.

He pulls the pillow gently away and reveals my hiding place. "Would you like to come out now?" he asks, and holds out his arms. I crawl out of the pillows. I am so happy to be hugged that I don't even realize I am crying until his shirt is all wet in a big circle.

When I apologize for messing up his shirt, Dad grins and says, "Now I know what a tissue feels like." It's a stupid joke, but you can't very well expect someone who has no sense of humor to all of a sudden be a comedian. So I smile anyway. I ask Dad if I can rest here on the sofa while he works. He hands me a throw blanket and I snuggle in. I don't say it aloud, but I don't want to go upstairs tonight.

Dad must understand that somehow because he leaves me there to sleep all night. I don't dream at all.

🌹

The next morning, Mom wakes me up for school. She is already dressed and ready, and she reeks of smoke. I follow her into the kitchen. Mom turns off the coffeemaker and pours herself a cup. I stare at the cans of protein drinks on the counter. They have extra calories in them, extra calories that are like poison to Lizzie. I know she won't even take a sip.

"How's Lizzie?" I ask immediately.

"I think she ate a little bit," my mother tells me with a tiny smile that doesn't reach her eyes. *When was the last time she really looked happy, instead of fake happy?* I can't remember.

Suddenly my mother reaches out and pulls me to her. Tight. Like everything in the world depends on this hug.

Then, just as suddenly, she releases me. "Did you study for your spelling test?" she asks.

And just like that, we are back to business. *"Mmm-hmm,"* I lie. There's no big breakfast today, just a bowl of oatmeal with raisins. I devour the entire bowl and drink two glasses of orange juice.

After I get dressed in the downstairs bathroom, I make my way to Lizzie's room. I knock softly and then push open the door. She's still on her bed, in the same position as last night. I forget once again about her thorns and long to hold her.

"Hey," I offer.

"Hi," she answers in a crackly voice.

"I have to go to school," I begin, but Lizzie cuts me off with a harsh witchy laugh.

"Of course, gotta have that perfect attendance record, right?" Her tone is sarcastic and bitter and it send chills down my legs. This isn't the Lizzie I know.

"I'm so surprised they aren't sending me. Except then people would know that we aren't perfect. Then Mom would be so disappointed." She's so angry.

I am frozen in place. *Who is this person? Where's my Lizzie?* Straight-A student, homecoming queen, my idol.

"I learned some new diet tricks in the hospital. I'll show you when you get home."

I am horrified. I don't want to hear any more. I want to run. Hide. I turn and flee. Happy, for once, about my perfect attendance record.

The next three months pass in a blur. I don't notice anything. I am a robot, going through the motions. Walk to class. Sit in my seat. Open the book. Answer questions. Walk to next class. Sit in seat. Lunchtime. Bite. Chew. Swallow. Soccer practice. Catch ball. Drop ball. Kick ball.

Until Tuesday, June 6. I have a nightmare. I'm in a river, and Lizzie is trying to swim toward me, but the churning water keeps pulling her under. I can't reach her. I try and try. And then she slips out of my hands. I dive underneath the surface, but I can't see anything. Just like that, Lizzie disappears. And the water goes still. I wake up shaking. My clock reads 3:20 A.M. I lie there awake. Afraid to close my eyes.

I hear the door from the bathroom open. Bare feet on the carpet. And then the cool air as my covers are pulled back. Lizzie slips into bed beside me. I roll over to face her. I can just barely see her face in the milky light.

"I heard you call out," Lizzie whispers. "Did you have a bad dream?"

I nod.

Lizzie reaches out her hand and gently strokes my cheek. "Do you want to talk about it, J?"

I shake my head. I don't want to share this nightmare with Lizzie. It might scare her.

"Remember when we were little and had bad dreams, and Mom would sing to us?" she asks.

Then she starts singing softly. "Hush little baby, don't say a word, Mama's gonna buy you a mockingbird. And if that mockingbird won't sing, Mama's gonna buy you a diamond ring . . ."

I join in. "And if that diamond ring turns brass, Mama's gonna buy you a looking glass. And if that looking glass gets broke, Mama's gonna buy you a billy goat." We keep singing to the end of the song. And then we look at each other and laugh. Not for any reason. But just because we feel like it. Then I reach out and take Lizzie's hand in mine. It feels so cold. So fragile. Like a baby bird. I hold it carefully. Gently. And we go to sleep.

When I wake up in the morning, Lizzie is back in her room, scribbling away in one of her notebooks. I get dressed and go to school. All day long, I feel like I am swimming against the current. Just trying to stay afloat.

Zoe's mom drives me home after school. I am looking out the window, but not really paying attention to anything. We turn the corner, and instantly, everything comes into focus in Technicolor. I see the red lights flashing. My father's blue Volvo home too early. The emerald-colored hose still running near the fuchsia petunias. My mother's lemon gardening hat on the steps.

By the time we get to the driveway, my mouth has gone totally dry. I fling open the door before the car is stopped. I run up the drive past the paramedics' van. My mother stands in the doorway. Her face is frozen. Her mouth hangs open in an *O* shape. My father is speaking with two men in uniforms. I dash for the stairs, but a paramedic stops me with a hand on my shoulder.

"Sorry, miss," he tells me, "but you can't go up there just yet."

I look from my father to my mother. My mother to my father. *What's happening? Where's Lizzie?*

"I'm so sorry, sir," the paramedic in charge is saying to my father. I can't take my eyes off this man's mouth. It's like he's speaking in slow motion and I hear it on a loud-speaker. "We'll know more after the autopsy."

I still don't understand what's going on. I pull on my father's suit jacket.

"Daddy, where's Lizzie? What's wrong with Lizzie?" I ask in a panic.

My father notices me for the first time. His eyes squint at me as though he doesn't recognize me. "Honey, I'm so sorry," he begins.

I dash for the front steps again. "Where's Lizzie? I want to see Lizzie," I scream. But the paramedic won't let me through. He blocks my way. I try to push him aside. But he's much bigger than I am. He doesn't budge.

"Let me see my sister!" I scream. My father wraps his arms around me from behind and lifts me up. He turns me around. I see my mother in the doorway, still wearing the *O*.

"Honey, she's gone."

And that's the last thing I remember.

Chapter 6

We are the house of the living dead. Glassy-eyed, silent, invisible. We move through the rooms without looking at one another, as if somehow this will make it all hurt less. The last time we touched was when my father told me Lizzie was dead.

In the twenty-four hours since then, the following things have happened:

1. The autopsy confirmed that Lizzie died from ingesting too many laxatives and diuretics—both of which she got from my mother's medicine cabinet.

2. A funeral has been planned for Friday.
3. I got to stay home from school for two days, which is a good thing since I can't stop crying.
4. My grandparents arrived, which isn't really so bad. My mom's mom is a little too type-A neurotic for me, but my grandpa (who isn't really, because my grandpa died when I was three) just sits in a chair and he can't hear anything at all since he refuses to wear his hearing aid. They're sleeping in my room, which is okay because even though I am supposed to be sleeping in the den, I have been sleeping in Lizzie's bed for the last two nights.

I read through every one of Lizzie's journals. Twice. Then I hid them in a pillowcase underneath my bed. Because I know Lizzie wouldn't want my parents to read them. They're filled with dark, angry feelings. It's a side of Lizzie they should never know. But at the same time, I can't bring myself to destroy them. Not when she poured herself into these notebooks. They're the only piece of Lizzie I have.

Right now I am sitting in the backyard on the old hammock. I am using one foot to push it back and forth, back and forth. It's my favorite time of day, just before sunset, when the sky is all hazy and golden, and the air is still. I can smell jasmine.

I feel so many things right now. Mad. Guilty. Frustrated. Scared. Sorry. But most of all—sad. I don't know what to do with the large open space where my heart used to be. It seems like no matter how much I cry, I never run out of tears.

My family is Presbyterian. Not super-religious Presbyterian. Just your average go-to-church-on-holidays and sometimes when Mom remembers that it's Sunday morning. Not religious enough to give me answers to all this. Just enough to confuse me. Like what kind of God allows a beautiful teenager to die. And why her?

I can't stop remembering things about Lizzie. Things no one but me would know. I lie back and see Lizzie holding my hand, helping me to walk in high heels, both of us dressed in my mom's evening gowns with rhinestone necklaces and elbow-length gloves. I remember how she would always let me wear the pink dress because pink was my favorite color—even though she loved it just as much. I remember her brushing my hair for hours after it would get all knotted at the beach. I remember the two of us lying on the floor in the den, watching our favorite movies and sharing a bowl of popcorn.

Most of all, I remember her smile. She smiled at me in a way that only Lizzie could do. It began like a sunrise with the curling of her lips and spread over her face like the morning sun until the rays couldn't stand to be contained any longer and had to spill out of her eyes. They would sparkle at me, and I felt like I was basking in her sunshine.

I don't know how I'm supposed to live without her.

I feel so alone. I want to be with her. I leave the hammock and enter the house. I climb the staircase to her empty room. The door is open. I peek inside. My mother is sitting on the bed, a pile of Lizzie's clothes next to her.

She looks so thin. And even though her hair is perfectly combed and she's dressed in a matchy-matchy outfit, she is a mess—lost and empty.

"Mom?" I ask tentatively.

She looks right at me, but it seems like she doesn't see me.

"It's not the way it's supposed to be," she says flatly.

I don't know what to say.

"A mother isn't supposed to bury her child," she explains. "I'll never see her graduate high school, go to college, get married, have babies of her own." She breaks down at this last part. She's sobbing so hard I think I should go get my dad. I've never seen her like this before. And it terrifies me.

I put my arms gently around her and she leans into me. For a moment, I feel the weight of her grief. It's overwhelming.

"Should I get Dad?" I ask her quietly.

She shakes her head no. Then she pulls back from me and wipes her tears away. She takes a couple of jagged breaths.

"I'm all right now," she tells me.

"What are you doing with her clothes?" I ask. I realize that I am unable to say my sister's name aloud.

"Choosing a dress for her to wear."

Oh. A dress for Lizzie to wear. In her coffin. *What does it matter!* I want to scream. But it does matter—to Lizzie. She's watching me right now. And it matters to her.

I know exactly what dress she wants to wear. It's short and tight and black and my parents forbid her to ever wear it out of the house. I know this is what Lizzie wants to wear for eternity.

Wordlessly I hand the dress to my mother. I know she recognizes it—but she doesn't say anything. I kiss her on the cheek and then leave the room. I can feel Lizzie smiling. And this makes me happy, just for a split second.

The day of the funeral is the most gorgeous sunny day. June 9. Usually in Southern California, we get fog in June and we don't see blue sky until at least 2 p.m., but today is special. The sun shines for Lizzie.

I am wearing a black dress my mother bought me yesterday. I didn't have anything suitable, she said. I didn't go with her to buy it. She picked it out all by herself. I think it's perfect to be in this stiff, new black dress that doesn't feel like me. Because I don't feel like me. I feel like someone else today. This is happening to someone else. Someone else is burying her big sister.

I come down the stairs in a trance. I can feel how frozen my face is. I've never noticed that before—feelings in my face. Right now it's the *only* thing I feel. My grandparents are ready. Seated on the couch side by side. They got dressed early so I could have my room. My grandma's lily perfume mixes with grandpa's aftershave. The smell makes my head spin and reminds me how empty my stomach is.

I sit down in a wooden chair in the corner of the living room. I don't think anyone has ever sat in it before.

My mother comes downstairs in a black suit. I have to say she looks really beautiful, except for her eyes, which are all red and swollen.

"Does anyone want breakfast?" she asks in her "company" voice.

"Joseph and I already ate," my grandma tells her.

"Jane?" mother asks.

Food? Not a chance. Not today. I shake my head. *No.*

"Very well then. I'll be outside," she says.

Having a cigarette, I finish in my head. But today, for some reason, I don't feel angry about it. Today, I wish I had something to do that would make me feel better. Then suddenly I remember my birthday gift. The camera still upstairs in its box.

"Be right back," I tell them as I dash upstairs to my bedroom.

I almost collide with my father, who has just come out of his room in a black suit and dark gray tie.

"Sorry," I say breathlessly. "Forgot something."

The boxes sit under my dressing table. I'm not even sure how to load the memory card. I take the camera out of the box and flip the on switch. Then I grab the instruction booklet and turn to the page labeled *Getting Started.* I find the tiny latch on the back and pop open the door. The SD card slides neatly onto the slot. Then I gently close the door. I line up the white dots and screw the lens on tight. I push open the battery slot and slide the rechargeable battery in. I hope it comes charged. Then I turn the switch to "on." When I hear the soft whir of the camera motor, I know I have succeeded. I slip the camera into its case and sling the bag over my shoulder.

Just as I reach the door, I turn back. I grab my favorite

teddy bear, the one I have cherished my whole life—Tuffy. He was Lizzie's present to me when my parents brought me home from the hospital. He means safety, warmth, love. I mush him on top of the camera and zip the bag closed. The top bulges, but no one will notice. Then I head downstairs to meet my parents.

The funeral is at our church. Lizzie's picture sits in a big gold frame at the entrance. She looks gorgeous in it. The church is dank and musty in the morning heat. The sickly sweet smell of too many roses hangs heavy in the still air. We're really early, but some of my parents' friends are already there. My dad's mother, Grandma Tina, and some of her friends. People from Dad's office. Kids from school. Friends of Lizzie's. Teachers. I see Zoe and her mom as I pass down the aisle. She reaches out and squeezes my hand. I can't squeeze back because I am numb.

Ahead of me, I see Lizzie's coffin. I step up to the platform and look inside the mahogany box. She doesn't look like my Lizzie. She looks like a wax figure of Lizzie. She's in the tight black dress, only it doesn't seem so tight anymore. Her hair is long and smooth and golden. Her skin is too powdery. Her lips too red.

How can this be my sister? I was just lying in bed with her, singing lullabies. I feel my throat suddenly start to clamp shut, and I force myself to breathe through my nose. *Breathe in love, breathe out sadness. Breathe in Lizzie, breathe out pain.* If I had known I wasn't going to get to talk to her again, I would have said so much more. I would have told her all the things I loved about her. All the things I would never forget about her. Now all I can do is stare at this empty body where Lizzie used to be.

She's so alone. I'm suddenly afraid for her. Then I remember Tuffy. I unzip my bag and remove him. I give my bear a quick squeeze and then slide him next to Lizzie, just touching her left hand. "He'll watch over you, Lizzie." *And then a piece of me will always be with you.* As I begin to zip up my bag, I glance down and see the camera. Before I think about what I am doing, I whip it out and start shooting pictures of Lizzie.

Dead Lizzie. Her face. Her crossed arms. Her delicate hands with nails painted pale pink. Her mouth sewn shut, the little threads like bugs crawling through her lips, like they will once her body is in the ground. I keep shooting. I am beyond all thought. Incapable of restraint.

A hand clamps around my wrist. Tight.

"Ouch!" I shout.

"Put the camera away, Jane," my father says in The Voice. "Now."

I obey. I always obey. Like a well-trained dog. Roll over, Jane. Sit, Jane. Stay, Jane. Be quiet, Jane. Disappear, Jane.

Without letting go of my wrist, though loosening up a little, my father leads me to the first pew and sits me down next to my mother. She is a complete basket case. Now way beyond not letting anyone see her cry, she is all-out bawling.

The minister says a few words and then some of Lizzie's friends stand up to read poems they have written. One of her teachers talks about what a wonderful student Lizzie was. Some of the cheerleaders get up and tell anecdotes about Lizzie at football games.

It's a funeral for the Lizzie that the world knew, but not the real Lizzie. I know they are speaking, but I have tuned them out. Until Dad stands up and walks to the podium.

As he begins to speak, I am suddenly more focused than I have ever been in my life.

"Elizabeth was the perfect child," he begins. I know this is about Lizzie. I know that she is dead, and that I shouldn't be thinking about myself at a time like this. But I can't help it. Because I know I am so not perfect.

"She was always so good at everything. And it came so

easy to her. We believed there was nothing she couldn't do. I had such high . . ."

He looks at my mother and suddenly he loses it. He chokes and sobs. We all sit silently, waiting for him to go on. But he can't seem to continue. Finally, he manages to speak again.

"I had such high hopes for her. Such dreams for her. She was so perfect, we just couldn't believe anything could ever be wrong with her. And that was our biggest mistake. My biggest mistake."

He sobs again. "Because she needed my help. And I let her down."

Then he looks right at me. "I let us all down."

Now it is my turn. I have asked to read one of Lizzie's poems. I don't think I could have actually spoken out loud about how I feel or how much I will miss her. It's too personal. I don't want to share it with a roomful of people. But I want people to remember that Lizzie had feelings. That she was human. And her writing will do that.

I copied the poem word for word out of one of Lizzie's notebooks. Now I clutch that precious single sheet of paper in my hand as I take the podium.

"This is a poem that Lizzie wrote," I whisper. "It's called 'Imprisoned.'"

I stare out at all the faces. Some people are weeping softly, others hug one another. My eyes drift over them, barely recognizing any of them. And then I spot Zoe. Zoe. Her amber eyes urge me on. I stay with her and begin to recite the poem.

"Sometimes I can't breathe for the pain
boring like leeches into my heart
The screaming voice of destruction
silently assaults my ears
Blocking out waterfalls,
children's laughter,
the song of the lark
And I am imprisoned

"The sunlight dances across my nose
But I am shrouded in darkness
For every day I mourn my own demise
And every day I will crawl
from my shelter of blankets
and do it all again
For I am imprisoned

"How I long to be free of this weight
To have wings that I could fly into tomorrow

Instead I dwell in a cave of impossibility
Where dreams are dead but not forgotten
and failure is the inevitable truth
Always I am imprisoned."

I finish in a strong voice. Without crying. The room is still. Silent.

I realize they are all staring at me. I instantly lose whatever poise I had. I look down at the crumpled paper in my hand and stumble off the podium. I slide back into my seat without looking at Mom or Dad. But Dad reaches for my hand. He grips it tightly and squeezes. I don't let go.

The minister begins to speak. He talks about ashes and dust. But I am not listening anymore. It's now like a movie on fast-forward. The minister's mouth is moving, but I hear no sound. I am there, but I am not there. The next thing I know we are standing. Getting into the car. Driving.

Now we are at the gravesite. An enormous gaping hole in the ground leers at me. Cut into the crayon-colored green grass, it looks black and dark and cold. The June sun beats down onto my back through the black dress. I can feel my temples start to sweat. My hair is so heavy; I want to shave it off right now. Be bald.

My mother is weeping. My grandmother is sobbing.

I hear sniffles and nose blowing from the hundreds of people gathered around us. I am a statue. Frozen. The coffin is closed now. I can't see Lizzie anymore. One by one we step forward to lay roses on top of the coffin. My parents go first. When it's my turn, I choose a lavender rose.

"I love you, Lizzie," I whisper as I kiss the rose gently and lay it on the shiny surface.

I think, *I am doing okay*. I think, *I am stronger than I thought*. But something happens when they start to lower the box into the ground. I stop breathing. I start to gag. The tears blind me, and I know that Lizzie needs me with her.

"Lizzie!" I scream. Someone grabs onto me. And I melt into the ground.

Chapter 7

When I open my eyes, I'm lying in my bed at home. Someone has taken off my shoes and put them neatly, side by side, next to the bed. I'm still in the black dress.

"Jane." I hear a gentle voice.

Zoe has come upstairs. I turn my head and see her sitting on the edge of my bed.

She wraps her slender arms around me and holds me tight. I feel her warmth touching me, and I want to grab onto it and take it in. But I can't hug her back. My arms remain pinned to my sides. Zoe understands. Because she's Zoe.

"Come on," she says softly, and we head downstairs hand in hand.

I see people mingling around. Some I know. Many I don't. *How can people stand around eating big spoonfuls of tuna salad?* I wonder.

Misty is standing with Zoe's mother. She reaches out and hugs me. Then Zoe's mother pulls me to her. They murmur words of sympathy, and I nod in return. My thoughts and feelings float through me like wisps of fog. They touch down and then lift off before I understand them. All I know is that if I stand still, the emotions will come pouring out of me like a torrential downpour. So I whisper a thank you, and keep moving.

I drift through the sea of bodies and bits and pieces of conversations touch my ears.

"Such a beautiful girl."

"What a tragedy."

"Anorexia is so misunderstood."

"Some people say she did it on purpose."

I stop dead in my tracks and whirl around, looking for the speaker.

"It was an accident," I shoot back when I spot her.

The woman turns ghostly white. I recognize her as the mother of one of Lizzie's friends.

"My sister never would have killed herself!" I shriek. I don't notice at first that the room has gone completely silent. That everyone is staring at me.

I have no clue what to do next.

A warm hand touches my shoulder. I turn.

There is a woman standing next to me. She has a black, chin-length bob tucked behind one ear. She smiles at me. Her eyes are warm behind her thin wire-rim glasses.

"I'm Dr. Patricia," she explains in a soft but clear voice. "Lizzie's therapist."

I know that since her first visit to the hospital, Lizzie had been seeing a therapist. But I didn't expect her to be here.

"Come with me," she says quietly but firmly. I obediently follow her from the room. As we cross the threshold from the dining room into the kitchen, I can hear the hum of conversation start up again.

Dr. Patricia opens the French doors leading from our kitchen to the patio. Happy to be outside, I gulp in fresh air hungrily. She seats me gently in one of the cushioned wicker chairs next to the lemon tree. Dr. Patricia takes the other chair and pulls herself close. Our knees are almost touching as we face each other. Neither of us speaks at first.

"I've thought of you often," she starts.

"Me, really?" I say stupidly. "How come?"

"Because you are the one everyone forgets about at a time like this."

I listen.

"When one sibling sucks all the energy out of a family, it is the remaining sibling who suffers the most. The forgotten one."

I nod, not really sure if I think she's right or not. Sometimes I did feel angry at Lizzie—everything was always about her. But right now I don't want to be mad at her.

"I should know. My sister was an anorexic," she tells me. "She overcame the disease and survived. My family is so grateful. But no one ever noticed how difficult her illness was for me. No one noticed me at all." Dr. Patricia leans in and looks deep into my eyes. I can smell her perfume, only it's sort of cologny. Citrusy and fresh. "If you need to talk, please call me. Don't try to do this all on your own. No one can."

I nod again. I haven't spoken at all, but it's not necessary. Dr. Patricia smiles a sad smile.

"It gets better. You'll never stop hurting and missing Lizzie, but you'll find a way to live with the pain. You are stronger than you know. She admired that in you."

Dr. Patricia stands and drifts back through the doors into the kitchen. *Lizzie admired something about me? Me?* Suddenly I just want to be upstairs in Lizzie's room. I slide through the living room. No one bothers me. They probably all think I'm psychotic.

I climb into Lizzie's bed and bury my face in her pillow. It still smells a little bit like her shampoo. Like roses. I pull the covers up over my head.

And there I weep. For my sister. For myself. And then I fall asleep.

Chapter 8

By Monday morning, everyone is acting normal. *Acting normal*. No one *feels* normal, but we're all good at pretending in the Holden house. It's more comfortable.

Chocolate-chip pancakes and chicken-apple sausage. Grandpa is the only one who eats.

I'm supposed to go back to school today. After all, there's only a week and a half left before summer vacation. Dad is driving me. So when he stands, I grab my cleats and peck Mom and Grandma on their cheeks.

"See you later," I mumble.

I pretend to study in the car. It's better than talking. But after a few minutes, Dad interrupts me.

"I was thinking maybe we should go on a vacation this summer," he says.

"Really?" I respond. I don't want to go on a vacation without my sister.

"Maybe to a dude ranch, or on a cruise to Alaska . . ." he tries.

Now I have to laugh.

"Dad, do you even know how to ride a horse?" I ask as he pulls up in front of school.

"Well . . ." He clears his throat. "Not exactly. But how hard can it be?"

I lean over to give him a hug.

"A-plus for effort, Dad," I tell him.

And then I go to school.

It's hard to be there. Knowing everyone knows. They look at me funny. Like they feel sorry for me. And that makes me feel worse. I wish they would just pretend they didn't know.

Zoe and Misty are amazing. They act normal. Sharing lunches and chitchatting as always. Zoe is going to tennis camp the week after school lets out. She'll be in Florida all summer. Misty is being shipped off to summer school in Switzerland, which she's not really looking forward to. I'd switch places with her in a nanosecond. Other than Dad's very-strange-and-not-likely-to-come-to-fruition vacation plans, I'm stuck at Casa Holden 'til September. And it's not a pleasant thought.

I try my best on my final exams, but I know my grades are going to be worse than ever this year. I wish I could be like Lizzie and get A's without trying. But I'm still me— B's and C's are my destiny. My parents can't say anything about it. Usually I would receive at least two days' worth of lectures about being more serious, trying harder . . . being more like Lizzie. But this time, my mother passes the report card to my father without a word. He just nods.

"Good job, Jane," my mother says.

They wish they still had Lizzie. If they had to lose one daughter, I'm sure they rather it had been me. Average Jane. Not Exceptional Elizabeth.

Zoe's mom invites me to a yoga class. I don't want to go. But it's our last chance to take a class together before Zoe leaves for camp. So I agree. When Zoe's mom picks me up, I slide into the backseat, and, for a second, everything feels normal. Here I am in this messy minivan, with the music blaring, on my way to yoga. And for a little while, I can fool myself.

When we get to the yoga studio, Zoe's mom takes her place at the front of the room.

Zoe and I pick spots on the bare wood floor and roll out our yoga mats. Mine is amethyst. Zoe's is emerald green. We sit down cross-legged on our mats and begin breathing slow and even. *Breathe in, breathe out,* I tell myself. I feel my breath warm my lungs. I fill them up to capacity, then let the air out really slow. Up and down my chest moves. It feels good to focus on something other than tears. I coach myself silently.

Breathe in love, breathe out pain. Breathe in peace, breathe out pain. Breathe in . . . I lose focus. Around us, the class is arranging their mats. In a few moments, Zoe's mom welcomes the group and then asks us to begin by centering our breath. I breathe in and out again, even and slow. Then we begin the poses. We do downward facing dog, where we bend at the waist and put our hands on the ground, creating a triangle shape. It feels good to stretch my legs out long. I feel the pull in the back of my calves. Zoe's mom presses on my back slightly to deepen the pose. I stretch into the pull.

"Breathe," she coaches me.

Then we drop into child's pose, where we crouch on the ground with our chests pressed against our knees and our foreheads touching the mats. Cobra has us lying on our stomachs, stretching our chests into the air, like snakes about to strike. Then back into downward-facing dog.

Later, we stand up for my favorite, tree pose. This pose has us standing on one leg, with the other one bent so that our foot touches our knee, hands raised as if in prayer over our heads. It's really hard to balance on one leg, but when I really focus, I can do it. And I love the feeling that I can work my body into these positions and hold them. We move slow and steady and Zoe's mom reminds us to breathe and not to worry about how we are doing compared to someone else.

"Yoga is not a contest," she reminds us. "It's a process. This is a journey you take with your mind and your body working together. Trust your body and where you need to be today."

I breathe and concentrate on my body. And I try to live in the moment. I do a good job. Until the part of the class where we have to sit cross-legged and close our eyes. This is the part where we're supposed to focus on the light in the middle of our foreheads.

Only when I focus on the light, all I see is Lizzie. She's

wearing a long white flowing gown and she's waving to me. Her hair is loose around her, falling over her shoulders in soft waves. A pale golden light surrounds her. I want to touch her, but she floats just beyond my reach. I keep trying, but I can't reach her. I cry out.

Someone touches my shoulder. I open my eyes. Zoe's mother kneels beside me.

"Jane, breathe."

I nod and take a deep breath. I know she knows I have been thinking about Lizzie. I can see it in her eyes. But she doesn't say it. And neither do I. But I feel one tiny tear slip out of the corner of my eye. It sears my skin as it falls down my cheek and drips off my chin onto the mat. I look at the little droplet. Shiny on the amethyst mat. And then I wipe it away with my bare foot. I watch the smear evaporate. And then it is gone. Like it never happened.

We all open our eyes and bring our hands together, palms touching in front of our chests. Then we bow to Zoe's mom and say *"Namaste."* It's an Indian greeting that is a way of honoring one another. It also signals the end of class. I roll up my mat slowly. *Nothing is the same anymore,* I think. *I used to love yoga.* Now I'm not sure I ever want to come here again.

🌹

On the way home, I am quiet. Zoe munches trail mix. Zoe's mom turns down the radio.

"Jane, you're welcome to come to class anytime this summer, even when Zoe is away. I'd love to see you." Her tone is light, but I know Zoe's mom is worried about me. Normally, this would make me feel warm and happy inside. But right now all I feel is empty. So I respond mechanically. It's all I can do.

"Thank you."

When they drop me off at home, Zoe grins at me.

"I'll see you tomorrow. I'm wearing my new bikini."

I manage a small smile. Tomorrow Misty's mom is having a going-away party for her. There's going to be swimming and ice-cream sundaes, popcorn and hot-dog vendors; even a DJ. Zoe has been planning her wardrobe for a week. I haven't even decided if I'm going. But I haven't got the energy to tell her that—or to see the look of disappointment on her face when she hears I'm not going to be there with her.

"See you," I say, and close the door.

By morning, I have decided to go to the party, just for a little while. After all, it is my last chance to say good-bye to Misty and Zoe. I choose an old bathing suit from last year. It's a purple one-piece with bright blue zigzags. I pull on a pair of blue-and-white board shorts and a white T-shirt. I smooth my hair back into a ponytail. Then I slather sunblock all over my face and body. Don't want to get any more freckles.

When I am ready, my mom drives me over to Misty's house.

I synchronize my red diving watch to the clock in Mom's car. "Come back in exactly one hour," I tell her.

"Why don't you call me," she suggests. "You might be having a good time."

"One hour," I say before I shut the door.

Misty's house is really fancy. Her mom has all these white gauzy canopies hanging over the lounge chairs. Stone statues peeking out from rosebushes. They even have a pond with floating lily pads and those oversize goldfish with the big gaping mouths. Misty has invited the entire sixth grade class. Everyone is swimming and eating ice cream. Even Kirsten Mueller and her henchgirls are here. I don't take off my shorts or T-shirt. I just sip a soda and plaster that fake smile on my face again. I drift around the party pretending to have a good time. No one notices. At least that's what I tell myself.

I'm looking at the fish in the pond when suddenly I notice my reflection. It surprises me. Because I don't look like me. At least not the me I think I am. I look like someone has put a mask over my face, and now I am "sad girl." I stare at this stranger and I wonder if I like her. I can't decide. My body aches, and I want to go home. I check my watch—only fifteen minutes to go.

I find my friends to say good-bye. Misty wants me to stay longer. She tells me her mom will drive me home later. Zoe says the same. But the truth is, I want to go home. I hug both of them and tell them I will miss them. I see a cloud of worry pass over Zoe's eyes, and I rush to leave before she says anything.

"I'll e-mail you," I promise. And then I hurry out the back gate to the street. I sit on the grass in front of the house and wait for my mom. As soon as her car drives up, I climb in and close the door.

"Did you have a good time?" she asks.

"Yeah," I say. It's only a few minutes to our house. The silence in the car is deafening. I can't wait to get out.

As soon as I get home, I find myself in Lizzie's room. Again. I guess I just want to talk to her. I want to laugh with her. To share secret dreams with her. I want her to be with me. My sister, my best friend.

I sit on the floor and look at the pictures taped around

the mirror. Lizzie's Secret of Success. Her icons. I touch one of the photographs. She doesn't need these anymore, I think. And I tear one down. Then I reach for another. I feel a sick sort of pleasure when the tape sticks and the magazine photo rips in half. So I pull off another.

With an increasing fervor that both frightens and excites me, I proceed to destroy each and every photograph on Lizzie's wall of perfection. When I have all the photographs torn off, I stuff them into a trash can. I hurry to the kitchen for matches.

I take my contraband back to my room. And I light the trash can on fire. I burn each and every photo. Lizzie's dreams. Burning in a trash can.

I have to admit, I love watching the flames slip over the pictures, curling the edges and turning them black. It feels so good to watch them turn to ashes and disappear forever.

"Jane! Jane!"

My mother's voice wakes me from my trance. My parents must smell the smoke because they both come rushing into my room. But by the time they get here, only embers are left, glowing crimson at the bottom of the pink metal can. I reach in with one finger to touch them. To make sure that there is nothing left of Lizzie's secret. Ouch! I burn my finger. I pull it out of the ashes and see that it's covered with soot.

"What in the world is going on here?" my father demands.

"Jane!" My mother.

But I am unfazed. I shrug my shoulders. "Having a little bonfire. To herald the first day of vacation," I quip. My dad raises an eyebrow. Mom puts her hands on her hips.

They are both giving me the eye. Like they think I've gone mad. Straitjacket mad. I decide to ease their nerves.

"Don't worry, I'm not planning on burning the house down. I just wanted to get rid of a couple of things."

Dad spots the matches and swoops them up. "No more matches for you."

"Don't need them anymore," I tell him. "I'm all finished."

"Was that something of Lizzie's?" my mother asks me as my father reaches for the trash can.

I shrug. "Nothing important, Mother. Not to worry," I say with a harsher tone than I mean. My mother turns and walks out without another word. My father follows her.

And so my summer begins.

Chapter 9

On the first day of summer break, Mom has a new agenda. She doesn't get out of bed. She keeps the shutters closed and the covers up over her head.

Dad and I eat cereal. Instead of commenting on Mom's behavior or my pyrotechnics show yesterday, Dad sticks with the off-the-wall vacation game. We go back and forth throwing out new vacation ideas. Dad suggests a safari in Africa. I tell him I'd like to go ride ponies in Iceland.

Other than our jokes about outlandish summer vacations, the meal is silent. Just the sound of the spoons against the china. It's a very sad sound.

The silence gives me time to think. I think of Zoe on her way to tennis camp and Misty packing to leave for Europe. Grandma and Grandpa already home in Arizona. Mom's place sits empty. Lizzie's place sits empty. And even though we don't talk about it, I know we are both thinking about it.

I spend the entire day channel surfing. And eating. Everything I can get my hands on. Dad comes home early with Chinese food. Again, the two of us sit at the table. Dad offers me a trip to Disneyland. In Paris. I suggest scuba diving in Fiji. The rest of dinner is composed of the sound of plastic forks scraping on paper plates. I skip the fortune cookies and head right for bed.

The next day is my second day of summer. Yippee. Dad leaves early for a breakfast meeting. Mom doesn't get up again. So I sleep late. When I wake up at noon, I don't bother to get dressed. I fill a mixing bowl with every kind of cereal. Frosted Mini-Wheats, Fruit Loops, Cheerios, Special K, and some kind of organic whole-wheat diet cereal of Mom's. I pour a layer of sugar over the whole thing and drown it in milk. I take my trough into the TV room and settle into my new favorite spot. For I have found something to occupy my summer days—soap operas. I used to hate them with a vengeance, but things are different now. I'm different now. I feel better about my own life when I'm watching other people's lives fall apart. Even if I know it's all fictional.

By the end of day two, I am an official couch potato. Game shows, talk shows, music videos, my beloved soaps, even the occasional infomercial. I consume endless bags of chips, pints of ice cream, and licorice. I spend all day in my pajamas. I figure I have no reason to get dressed—I'm not going anywhere.

Mom stays in bed. She keeps the room dark and she refuses to speak to anyone. Not that I care. I'm happy with my snack foods and remote. The days move so slowly, sometimes I think time is standing still. Just to mess with me. I spend so many hours watching detergent commercials, I know all the ads by heart.

When I can't stand another minute of infomercials for exercise equipment, I drag myself up the stairs to my bedroom, where I sit in front of the mirror counting my freckles. I stack lint balls. And I eat. *A lot.* I won't go anywhere near the swimming pool or the bikes in the garage. I refuse to do anything fun—or even remotely amusing. I don't return Zoe's texts. I ignore Misty's e-mails.

Every night, when Dad comes home and sees Mom in bed, they have a fight. When she's still like that after a week, they have a gigantic fight. A World War–category fight. Their door is closed, so the words are muffled, but I can hear that they are angry. It's in the response time. When people are fighting, their words come quicker than when they are listening to one another. I creep out of my room and place my head against the door to listen.

"Just leave me alone," Mom begs. "I want to be left alone."

Dad sounds really mad. "What do you think is happening to Jane all day while you're hiding in bed? Do you know what she's been doing all week? Eating junk food. Oh, and watching soap operas. She doesn't even get dressed. You think that's a good way for her to spend her summer? We might as well just buy the coffin now. Because you're putting her in it. Just like you did to Lizzie."

When I hear Dad's words, I start to shake.

He thinks I am going to fall apart like Lizzie did? I would never do that. *I wouldn't.* But then I think about it. Isn't that what I have been doing all week? Staying in my pajamas, refusing to talk to my friends, eating myself sick. I've been acting like my mom. Like Lizzie.

"I want my Lizzie back!" she shrieks. Then, "Get out!"

Dad opens the door suddenly. And I jump back. I am embarrassed to have him find me there listening.

We stare at each other for a second. "I'm sorry you had to hear that," Dad tells me as he collects himself. I'm so surprised that he's not angry with me that I blurt out what I'm thinking.

"I'm not like Lizzie," I tell him.

"I know that," he tells me. And he gathers me in his arms and holds me tight.

I fall asleep in my own bed that night.

I wake with a start. My clock says 3 A.M. I'm soaking wet. I go into the bathroom to splash water on my face. That's when I hear something in Lizzie's room. I hurry over to the bathroom door and walk through to the adjoining room.

I am horrified by what I see. Packing boxes are in the center of the room. Mom is opening the closet and taking out Lizzie's clothes.

"What are you doing?!" I shriek.

Mom glances at me briefly as she lays the clothes on the bed. "Packing."

There is no emotion in her voice.

I step in front of her with my arms out to protect the clothes from further touching.

"You can't do that. These are Lizzie's clothes."

My mother sighs. "Jane. Lizzie doesn't need these clothes anymore. She's dead." Her voice is flat. "Other people can use these things."

My mother is going to give away Lizzie's things. I look at her like she is a complete stranger.

Mom turns back to the closet to pull out more hangers. My mind whirls, trying to think of something I can do to stop her. Anything.

And then I seize on it. "Does Dad know about this?" I say in my parent voice.

Mom freezes.

"I'm calling Dad," I threaten. Mom shrugs and goes back to her work.

I run down the hallway and into my parents' room. Only Dad isn't there. His side of the bed hasn't been slept in.

I run down the stairs, taking the steps two at a time. I find him sleeping on my sofa in the TV room. I shake him. "Dad, Dad, wake up!"

Dad opens his eyes. Squints at me. "Jane, what's wrong?" He asks. I can hear the fear in his voice.

"Mom's packing up Lizzie's room. She's going to give her things away."

He doesn't say anything. I wonder if he has understood

me. Then he speaks in a tight voice. "Jane, go to your room."

I return upstairs to my room and close the door. But I can still hear the fighting. Bits and pieces, when they're loudest.

My mother: "Well, you want me to move on. Here you go."

My father: "Not like this."

My mother: "That's easy for you to say. You're never home. You try spending all day in this tomb, walking back and forth in front of her door. And you know how much time Jane spends in here? God only knows what she'll burn next!"

Then everything goes silent. The next thing I hear is the door to Lizzie's room opening and footsteps in the hallway.

After the quiet settles over the house, I creep through the bathroom and open up Lizzie's door. The room is dark. I can still see the boxes in the center of the floor. The heap of clothes on the bed.

I gently pick up Lizzie's things and carefully hang them back in the closet. I fold her T-shirts and line them back up in her drawers. I pick up the boxes and take them out to the garage. Mom is outside in the dark, consoling herself with nicotine. We don't speak to each other. I go back inside and climb into bed.

Dad wakes me up at noon.

"I was wondering, *ahem* . . ." He clears his throat as though he's nervous. Nervous about what, I think. *Me?* ". . . if you'd like to go somewhere with me this morning," he finishes.

I look at him with raised eyebrows. "Not really, I've been waiting all week to watch Saturday-morning infomercials" is the answer on the tip of my tongue. But there's something in his eyes. And so instead, I shrug.

"Okay," I say. It's the best I can do right now. He seems to understand that.

Twenty minutes later, we're on the Pacific Coast Highway heading north. My dad is playing my favorite radio station, which I know he hates. It makes me soften a bit since I know it's just for me.

We don't talk. I don't ask where we're going. He doesn't tell me. Not that I care. I'm actually happy just to be out of the house. I gulp breaths of air. I fill my lungs with life. And I try to empty my brain of all thoughts. My heart still feels heavy in my chest like a sponge soaked with water. But I'm getting used to the fact that I can't do anything about it—that it just is.

Dad pulls off the highway near Santa Barbara. I see antiques stores, clothing shops, cafés. Everyone looks so happy and carefree. I wonder if they really are. I wonder if any of them didn't want to get up this morning.

Dad turns up a narrow road and weaves into the hills and away from the ocean. After a few minutes of checking his directions and turning right and left, he pulls up in front of a white adobe house with a red tiled roof.

"Here we are," he announces proudly.

All of a sudden I think of this kid, Dennis Randall. I used to hear Lizzie and her friends talk about him. One day, his parents decided he had psychological problems and they had these men come and take him away in a straitjacket, to one of those military schools where they break you down so they can build you back up. Even though this house looks like anything but a military establishment, the thought unnerves me anyway.

I get out of the car and follow Dad, slowly, to the front door. I hang back a bit, in case the straitjacket men come running out. I can hear a lot of dogs barking inside the house. Dad rings the bell. More barking. Then the door opens.

There's a small person standing in front of Dad and me. Blond curls frame her cherubic face. Round, sky-blue eyes stare at us. She can't be any more than five.

I instantly relax. Dad isn't sending me away. Behind the girl hovers a pretty blond mother with her hair swept back in a loose ponytail. She wears a denim shirt bearing embroidered puppies. She smiles at the two of us.

"Hi, you must be Harold. I'm Lillian. And this"—she picks the child up in her arms—"is Sophia."

"Hello," says Dad. "This is my daughter—"

"Jane," Lillian finishes for him. I suddenly have the face-burning sensation of having been discussed before, and behind my back. But there's absolutely nothing I can do about it. I manage a bit of a smile. For Sophia.

I wonder why we are here, with Sophia and Lillian. Until Lillian says, "Come on in and see the puppies."

Puppies.

But of course, puppies. Now the barking makes sense.

But a puppy? My mother doesn't do pets. Not even a goldfish. Too messy. Too much work. Dad seems oblivious to this fact as he follows the woman into the other room. I see eight—no, nine—blond bits of fluff cavorting on the kitchen floor.

Sophia is set down by her mother and scampers into the fray like a puppy herself. She reaches for one of the pups and scoops it up gently. It licks her face with a petal-pink tongue. She holds the puppy out to me.

"This one is my favorite. Want to hold her?"

The old me would have already been on the floor, holding at least two puppies. But I'm not the same me anymore. I am the new me. So instead, I shake my head no. Sophia tosses her head and pouts a little, as if she can't understand why anyone wouldn't want to hold her favorite puppy. But I can't explain it to her. I can't even explain it to myself.

I remain near the door, watching. Dad sits on the floor in the middle of the puppies. He crosses his legs and the puppies tumble over them. He lifts them in the air one by one, bringing each one close to his face so he can look them in the eye. He talks to them softly. So softly that I can't hear a word he's saying. I've never seen my father like this. He seems so . . . fun. And nice. And relaxed. I notice then that he's not wearing a tie today. He's wearing a golf shirt with light blue stripes and jeans. *Jeans!* I didn't even know he owned jeans. He looks over at me and our eyes meet. He raises his eyebrows at me and holds up one of the puppies.

"Jane?" I shake my head. I can't. It's not that I don't want to touch one of the fluffy balls. *I do.* But I can't. It wouldn't be right to have fun.

And anyway, I don't want a dog. No one asked me. And I don't want one. A little tiny voice in the back of my head reminds me that I have *always* wanted a dog. I sweep the thought back into the far reaches of my mind with the other things I'd rather not think about.

An hour later, Dad and I are packed into the car with a puppy in a carrier, bags of dog food, and peepee pads.

"What's Mom going to say?" I ask as we pull back onto the Pacific Coast Highway and head for home.

Dad's jaw tightens. His eyes narrow and his voice is suddenly brisk. "It'll work out." Then he turns to look at me with a smile on his face. "Don't worry."

I'd like to believe him, except that I know Mom. And a golden retriever is not exactly a neat kind of dog. It's an energetic, jump-in-the-pool kind of dog. A muddy-feet kind of dog. And I know that this will not sit well with her.

Mom is in the kitchen when we get home. Still in her nightgown, but at least she's out of bed. Mom takes one look at the puppy, gives Dad a look of death, and stalks off to the garage without a word. I head up to my room. Dad is left to take care of the dog. It was his idea after all.

About an hour later, I make my way to the kitchen for a drink. I pass by Dad's study. The door is closed, but I can hear yelling from inside. I resist the urge to press my ear against the door and listen in. Still, I can't help hearing my mother's raised voice.

"But you know how I feel about animals."

And then my father's reply. "This isn't about you."

My mother suddenly flings open the door. I dash away just in time to avoid a collision. She runs out of the room and up the stairs. "Of course it isn't about me. It's never about me," she says.

I don't want Dad to catch me lurking in the hallway, so I hurry to the kitchen. The puppy crate is in the corner. I can see blond fur sticking through the slats in the side of the cage. I pour my juice and then step closer. I still haven't even touched the puppy. I can tell it's sleeping. It must be tired, I think. If the puppy knew about the trouble it had just caused, I'm sure it would want to go and live somewhere else. Anywhere else. I wouldn't blame it one bit if it hated the Holden house.

Chapter 10

When I wake up in the morning, the house is completely silent. It's not the silence of my parents sleeping, or even of everyone being outside. It's an absence of sound that makes my stomach clench and my adrenaline start to rush. It's stillness that can only mean one thing. I feel it in my bones.

Something is wrong.

I brush my teeth and pad down to the kitchen in my bare feet and cloud pajamas. The puppy watches me from her cage. I can see one brown eye peeking through the carrier.

"Hi," I say to her as I open the fridge for the orange juice. She just stares at me.

The silence is deafening. I have to get out. I head for the hammock and settle in.

My mind turns instantly to Lizzie memories. I remember one time we found a stray dog, a little white ball of curls. We fed it and bathed it. Dad put up signs around the neighborhood, but no one called to claim it. So, of course, we begged to keep the dog. We even named it. Cleo, after Clifford the Big Red Dog's best friend.

Mom said no. No dogs.

No dogs, no cats, no birds, no hamsters, no fish.

The vet said he would find a home for her. And just like that, Cleo was gone.

I realize suddenly that we don't have a name for this new dog. But it's not really right to give her a name when she won't be staying. I think about her, all alone in there. I wonder if she's scared. I wonder if she misses her brothers and sisters. Just then, Mom surprises me with a visit to the backyard.

"Hi," I say. I notice she is all dressed up in one of her church suits. Red with a strand of pearls around her neck. The red makes her look really washed out. She looks old. And tired. Really, really tired. Her mouth is all pinched around the edges, which usually means she's irritated about something. I smell cigarettes. The smell clings to her.

I decide not to speak first. I have no idea what I have done.

"I'm leaving," she says in a burst of exhaled air.

I don't know what this means. Is she going to church, to the grocery store, to the dry cleaners?

"I need a break. I'm driving to Arizona to visit your grandparents for a few weeks."

Okay. I'm processing this. Like what "a break" means. We all get to take breaks from school, from work. But do you get a break from your life? From your family?

My grandparents live in Sun City, Arizona, this retirement community located near the center of the earth. It's like 150 degrees there in the summer. You have to get up at five in the morning to do anything that doesn't involve air-conditioning. And the average age is ninety-eight—and a half. That doesn't exactly sound like a "break" to me.

Then it occurs to me. Maybe she needs a break from me.

"You can come if you want." She says this like she's obligated. Like she's obligated to like me. Even if she doesn't. I can tell from her tone that she hopes I won't actually take her up on it. Which I won't. Because as bad as my summer at home seems, Sun City sounds even worse.

"I'd rather stay here," I tell her flatly. *With Dad,* I think. But I don't say that part out loud.

She shrugs. "You'll be alone all day."

Like this is any different than it's been with her in the house. It might be better. At least there will be no pretense. "It's okay," I tell her.

Maybe this is the beginning of a divorce. Maybe this is how it happens. First, parents need a break. The next thing you know, it's all custody battles and court hearings. But right now I don't care. Actually, I am relieved. I know this sounds strange.

"I'll be leaving in an hour, if you change your mind," Mom tells me. She looks so weary. It makes me feel sad suddenly, like maybe I should go with her. Maybe she needs me. But she would never ever say that. It would be too honest. And honesty is not a virtue in the Holden house.

"Okay," I tell her. She clips into the house, her pumps clicking on the stone path. The discussion is over, just like that. I think again that maybe I should agree to go with her.

But I don't.

When Mom finally does leave, she calls me into the foyer to say good-bye. She hugs me really tight and kisses my cheeks. I can see tears in her eyes when she pulls away from me.

"*Be safe, Jane,*" she whispers. I nod. "I'll call you every morning," she promises. I nod again. That guilty feeling starts to bubble up again, making me feel hot and cold at the same time. Dad comes downstairs and Mom kisses him softly on the cheek. I can't read his expression at all. Mom shuts the front door with a soft click.

And then there were two.

Other than the exciting task of painting my toenails fluorescent green, the rest of the day is uneventful. I return to my room, and stay there, reading my camera manual for the fiftieth time. In the afternoon, Dad comes into my room carrying the puppy.

"Want to hold her?" Dad asks.

I look at this fluffy thing, with its wet black nose and big sad eyes.

I shake my head no.

"We could go out for ice cream," Dad suggests.

I shake my head again.

"Miniature golf? You used to love that."

"When I was five."

"Bungee jumping?"

That gets a smile. But just a teeny one.

"She still needs a name," Dad reminds me.

"Is she staying?"

Dad nods. "She's staying."

I consider the dog. "How about 'Kona'?" I offer.

Kona is the one place Lizzie and I always dreamed of visiting. Kona, Hawaii. When we grew up, we were going to build vacation homes there. Side by side on the same stretch of sand.

I don't know if we ever shared this dream with our parents—if we ever asked them to take us there for a vacation. So when Dad says thoughtfully, "Kona it is," I don't know if it means anything to him or not. Either way, the puppy has a name. And she's staying.

Dad orders pizza for dinner and we sit in front of the television while we eat. I don't mind. At least we don't have to fake-talk about things the way we did when we ate dinner "as a family." Then it hits me. We aren't a family anymore. Just a fragment of a family—the leftovers.

I also realize that this is the first time Dad and I have ever been on our own, just the two of us. And it's the first time we've ever eaten dinner in front of the TV. I wonder again if Mom and Dad are getting divorced. Maybe Mom is never coming back. Maybe this is just how it's going to be from now on. The thought makes me really, really tired. I tell Dad I'm going to bed. "I have to leave for an early meeting tomorrow," Dad tells me. "Will you be all right on your own?" he asks.

"No problem," I tell him.

"You're on puppy duty, then," he finishes.

"Okay." My mouth forms the words, but truthfully I'm not so sure. Kona is curled up in a little ball next to Dad's feet. She's looking pretty cute. But I still haven't held her.

"I'll write down how to feed her. She eats three times a day. Take her out before and afterward. And if you can, give her some time outside the crate. So she doesn't get too lonely."

"Okay, Dad," I mumble as I peck him on the cheek.

He pats my head. "Sleep tight, Little Bunny."

Dad hasn't called me "Little Bunny" since I was seven. Normally, this would really annoy me. But for some reason, right now I kind of like it.

The next morning, I open my eyes. And then it hits me. Today, I am a puppy sitter. I pull on some board shorts and a tank top and dash down to the kitchen. As soon as I open the kitchen door, I can hear the puppy scratching at her crate.

"Okay, okay. Hold on," I tell her as I try to get the latch open. I pull up the metal latch and the door swings open. Out she bounds. Covered in water. No, wait. She smells like a public bathroom. *Oh no!* She's covered in pee. She leaps on me, pressing both wet paws against my shirt.

"Great," I tell her. "Now we both need a bath." I am beyond annoyed. How could Dad do this to me? He was the one who wanted this puppy. Not me. And now I have to wash the crate, wash her, wash me, wash my clothes, and the kitchen floor.

I walk toward the door. Kona scampers beside me, eager to keep up, all the while making little puppy yipping sounds. When I open the door, she sees the grass and makes a dash for it. While she's sniffing around, I lean against the door frame. A whole day to myself. No one watching. Commenting. Criticizing. I can do anything I want today. Well, after I clean up Kona's mess. But after that, I can do anything I want.

The trouble is, I have absolutely no idea what that is.

It takes me almost an hour to clean up and feed Kona. I had no idea a puppy could eat so fast. I munch a bowl of cereal while she laps up her mushy puppy kibble. Mom calls. She rambles on with unimportant details about my grandparents. Things like "Your grandmother bought a new golf cart," and "The orthopedic shoes your grandfather tried really helped his gout." Oh, and "Did you know they have lots of classes here, like macramé and origami?" I tune her out after three minutes of this. Then Mom tells me she loves me, and we hang up.

Afterward, I take my camera and head outside. Kona follows me. She stays right behind my feet, no matter where I go.

I walk around the yard, snapping photos of the trees, flowers, a bird sitting on the fence. Even I have to admit, the pictures are kind of on the boring side. Just then, Kona dashes out from behind me. She's after a little white butterfly. The butterfly flits among the flowers, and Kona leaps in right after her. I start shooting: Kona splashing through the sprinklers. Kona leaping in the air to catch the butterfly. Kona tripping over the potted plants. Kona rolling in the grass. Kona collapsing in the shade, tongue hanging sideways out of her mouth.

All the while I am laughing. I can't help it. She's hysterical. She must be the most clueless puppy in the world. And she's adorable.

I fish a Popsicle out of the freezer and drop into the hammock. I use my left foot to push myself back and forth. Kona stands underneath, whining at me.

"What?" I ask her. "You want to come up?" She stops whining and stares at me with her big sad eyes.

"Okay," I agree. I reach down and swoop her up into my arms. I set her down near my leg. Only Kona has other ideas. She shimmies up next to my body and folds herself into my side. She places her head on top of my chest and closes her eyes.

And this is how I spend my first day alone.

Not alone at all.

That night, after Dad and I gorge on spaghetti and meatballs, I decide to download the photographs. I want to print some for Dad to see.

I take out the manual and turn to the pages about downloading pictures. First, I load the software. Then I attach the cable from the camera to my computer. The pictures start showing up, one by one.

My stomach churns. Suddenly those meatballs don't feel so good. My head spins. There's Lizzie in her coffin. The stitches holding her lips closed. The pallor of her skin.

I had forgotten. There are twelve of them. Twelve pictures of my dead sister. Twelve shots before my father stopped me, mortified at my conduct. And as much as I agree with him, I have to admit that I find the pictures fascinating. So fascinating that I print them out right away. I hold them in my hands. *Lizzie.*

Kona is curled up near my feet and I startle her when I jump up to stash the photos in my bedside table. I don't want Dad to see them by mistake.

By the time I take a look at the photos of Kona, I don't even feel like doing this anymore. I am so exhausted all I want to do is sleep. That's when Dad comes into the room.

"What's going on in here?" he asks in a friendly voice. I can't believe how different this Dad is from the Dad he used to be. The Dad I used to have didn't even look up from his papers when I came into the room. This Dad is coming into my room to see what I'm up to. Then it occurs to me. Maybe he *does* think I'm going to fall apart. Maybe he thinks I need special watching.

I quickly scroll down to the pictures of the puppy so as not to prove him right.

"I took some pictures of the puppy today. I wanted to surprise you."

Dad pretends to cover his eyes. "I won't look if you don't want me to."

"No, that's okay," I assure him. Dad reaches under me to pick up Kona.

"Looks like you two have bonded."

I raise an eyebrow. "You could say that."

"Was that before or after the pee fest?"

"Definitely after." I groan.

Dad leans in over my shoulder. "Hey, some of these are really good, Jane."

Dad's never complimented me on anything before. Not like this.

"Really?" I ask.

Dad nods. "You have a really good eye. That's something that can't be taught. It's the way you see things. Your shots have meaning. You see this one." He points to one of Kona splashing through the sprinklers. "This one has humor in it. It's funny. But this one." He gestures to one of Kona resting on the grass. "This one is quiet and thoughtful."

Dad swings around to look at me. "You are quite an artist, Jane Holden."

I beam. Inside and out.

"Which one is your favorite?" I ask him. I want to print one out for him.

"I think it would have to be this one." Dad points to a photo of Kona leaping in the air, the white butterfly just out of reach. "I like it for its infinite possibilities."

We smile at each other then.

The phone rings in the other room. While Dad goes to answer it, I slide some of the photo paper into the printer. I hit the print button. I am waiting for it to print out when Dad returns. He doesn't look happy.

"I have to fly to San Francisco tomorrow morning," Dad tells me. "It's a big client. No one else can handle it."

Oh.

"We'll just have to get a sitter for you."

A sitter! "Dad, seriously. I can stay by myself for a couple of days."

"It's three nights and four days. Either you have a sitter, or I put you on a plane to Sun City." *Geriatric sunbathing, here I come.*

I do my best negotiating. I even resort to whining. But Dad is not budging on this. I take a deep breath. I just had my first day of freedom and now it's all going to be ruined. Ruined by a babysitter. My every move will be watched, analyzed, reported. There has to be some argument, some angle. Then it hits me. I know how to derail this plan.

"Who?" I ask him sarcastically. I know for a fact that Dad has no idea where to find a babysitter.

Dad shakes a finger at me. "You think you're so smart," he says. "But I have a few tricks up my sleeve. I will find you a babysitter." And it's over, just like that.

One thing I can say for sure about my father, he is true to his word. Dad finds me a babysitter all right—the oldest woman on the planet, Mrs. Barnaby. She used to work as Dad's secretary until she retired. In addition to being the oldest woman on the planet, she's also the cheeriest. She's so happy that she makes you want to scream and rip your hair out.

I know it's going to be the longest four days of my life.

Chapter 11

When the doorbell rings the next morning at exactly
8 A.M., I am unprepared for the sight of her. Head-to-
toe purple. She's wearing shoes, drapey pants, and a large
caftan-type top—all in the same shade of ripe berry. She
has short, poufy white hair around which she has tied a
scarf in the same shade of—you guessed it—purple. I bet
even her underwear is purple. Not that I want to dwell on
the subject. Mrs. Barnaby is also large. Let's just say she is
a very big woman.

"Well, hi there, sugar plum," her voice kind of drawls.

And her smile, I have to admit, is infectious. I smile back.

"Hi, Mrs. Barnaby." I step back to clear a path. "Come in."

She carries a tiny little lemon-lime-colored Samsonite suitcase.

"Call me Ethel," she says. "We're going to have a good time together."

I bet, I think. *Break out the bingo boards.*

Kona dashes into the room, wagging her tail. "And who is this?" Ethel asks as she scoops the puppy up and plants a big wet one on her mouth.

Yuck.

"Kona," I tell her.

"Every family needs a dog," she says matter-of-factly.

"Well, in case you hadn't noticed, this family is down to one. Me."

She surprises me then. She sets Kona down gently and reaches out for me. She wraps me in the biggest bear hug. And she squeezes me tight.

"Darlin', your daddy's coming back. And your mama'll be back, too."

She pulls back then and looks at me. Real direct. Eye to eye. I notice that her eyes are sort of purplish. "And how are you doin'?"

"Fine," I tell her. My answer is on autopilot. And it's

the one I know people expect from me. No one wants to know the truth. That every morning when I open my eyes, my body has forgotten. For one brief second, I feel normal. But then, with the next breath, it all comes rushing back into me, like slamming headlong into a giant gray concrete wall. Or that the weight of it is so enormous that I can barely get up out of bed and put one foot in front of the other. *No one wants to know that.*

"I'm fine," I repeat.

"You said that," Ethel responds kindly. She tilts her head to the side and studies me. I feel like a specimen under a microscope. I look down at my feet.

"Well, I imagine at your age, you're not too happy about having a babysitter."

I look up at Ethel then. How did she know that?

She smiles at me. "I was young once, too. A very long time ago." She adjusts her purple scarf. "I'll just stay out of your way and let you do your thing," she promises.

I nod, happy at least that my babysitter is going to leave me alone.

I head outside to shoot some pictures of Kona. I toss a ball to her. She trips over her feet trying to catch it. I snap a shot. Then I follow her around and take pictures as she prances around the yard with the ball in her mouth.

Ethel keeps her promise and leaves me alone all morning. But at exactly noon, she calls me for lunch.

"I don't believe breakfast food is reserved for morning," Ethel confesses. "To me, breakfast food is comfort food. And comfort food can be eaten anytime you need some comforting."

So we have chocolate-chip pancakes for lunch.

It feels strange to be sitting at our table with a total stranger, instead of my parents and Lizzie. Now I have to be polite and make conversation.

"Thank you for the pancakes," I offer. They do taste really good, and I don't want Ethel reporting to Dad that I was rude.

"They're one of my specialties," Ethel tells me.

I expect to be asked questions, and to have to answer all these things about myself, like I am being graded. So I am surprised when Ethel starts to tell me about herself.

"I had a dog when I was your age," she begins. "Jack was his name. He was a mixed breed; a mutt, my mama called him. But I didn't care about that. He was perfect to me."

She gets a smile on her face as she remembers. I listen as I eat. It feels good to be somewhere else with my thoughts for a minute. I picture a young Ethel, dressed in a purple sundress, playing with a little brown-and-white puppy.

"You see, I was an only child. And my daddy, well, he left my mama and me when I was just a baby. So my mama had to raise me all on her own. And she had to work a lot. So I spent most of my time alone. Until I found Jack. Or rather, Jack found me."

I chew quietly and think about this. Ethel's life sounds really sad.

"Sometimes it's hard to understand why bad things happen," Ethel continues. "But I believe there's a reason for everything. Maybe it won't come clear to us right away, but I think if we remind ourselves that one day, we'll understand why, I think it makes it easier to get through the rough times."

I shrug. I've heard people say this before. But I'm not sure I believe it. After all, what could be the reason for Lizzie dying? What could ever make that okay?

"I see you're chewing that over, and I can see you have something to say about it," Ethel says. "Speak your mind, honey, there's nothin' to be afraid of. Except keeping things inside too long and letting them rot."

"I just don't believe everything happens for a reason. That's all," I tell her. It feels so strange to speak my mind like this. And scary, I have to admit. My stomach clenches as I speak, because I'm afraid I'm going to get in trouble.

But instead of Ethel getting mad at me, she puts her hands together and starts clapping.

"Bravo, darlin'. I love a good debate."

I realize that Ethel welcomes my disagreement. She applauds my honesty. And that feels good.

"I can't think of one reason, not one, why my sister shouldn't be here right now."

Ethel nods at me. She listens to me. And the shocking thing is that she doesn't try to change my mind. She doesn't try to convince me to hide my real feelings.

Then she says, "I would feel exactly the same way if I was you." She looks me directly in the eye. "I would be mad at the world. That's how I was when my husband died. Mad at everyone and everything."

I don't say anything. I just listen.

"I let myself stay mad for a long, long time. Until one day, I realized I wasn't mad anymore. I was just sad. And after a while, I wasn't sad anymore either. But I still miss him. And think about him every day."

"If everything happens for a reason," I say, "what was the reason your husband died?"

"I'm still working on that one," Ethel admits. "And one day, I'm certain I will understand it."

I take a long drink of milk and think about this.

Ethel smiles at me, gently, then. She reaches out and pats my hand. "Everyone deals with these things in their own way. You'll find your way. It just takes time."

After lunch, I decide to go swimming. Ethel follows me and sits down in a chair in the shade. She doesn't say anything. But instead of her presence annoying me the way I thought it would, it feels good to have someone nearby. It makes me realize how lonely I've been. Kona tests the water, but she's not ready to join me yet. Instead, she runs over to Ethel and jumps up, putting her paws on Ethel's lap. Ethel picks her up and holds her close. I climb out of the pool and grab my camera so I can shoot a picture of the two of them.

"This reminds me of my modeling days," Ethel tells me as she poses with Kona.

I try not to reveal my disbelief on my face. But it must show anyway.

"I know. You wonder how I could have been a model, seeing as I'm so enormous today," Ethel teases. "But I was. Oh, I was much younger then, and slimmer. I was a Breck girl." She tells me this proudly. I have no idea what this is.

Ethel realizes this. "You don't know what a Breck girl is, do ya?"

I shake my head no.

Ethel grins. "A Breck girl was a model for Breck shampoo. It was all-American, beautiful. Like Cover Girl is today."

Oh. "Lizzie used to hang magazine pictures on her mirror, of people she wanted to be like," I confess. "That's what started all the trouble."

Ethel smiles at me. "Wasn't the dream that caused the problem, darlin'. Was something inside of your sister. We live in a world filled with comparisons. We're always being compared. Asked to conform to a certain size, a certain weight, a certain beauty. But we have to learn to live with what's in here." Ethel taps her chest. "Because we live with it forever. Believe me, beauty fades. But who you are inside, that's who you can really depend on."

I think about her words. How can someone who looks so goofy be so completely profound? I wonder.

Dad calls to check in. I tell him that things are fine. And I really mean it. I can tell from his voice that he's relieved. At the end of the call, he tells me he loves me.

"I love you, too, Dad," I say. And a wave of emptiness washes over me. I feel so alone.

I walk through the house with Kona tagging at my heels. And I find myself wanting to look at something that reminds me of what my life was like. Before.

I head for the hallway closet. I pull it open and turn on the light. The Holden hallway closet is the place where things go when they don't belong anywhere else. There are old ski jackets, umbrellas, picture frames, Christmas decorations, photo albums, and cartons of things we can't throw away. I look for a box marked JANE in my mother's rounded handwriting. I find it on the back shelf, behind a pair of pink-and-white bunny slippers. I sit down on the floor and open the box. Inside are papers my mother has saved over the years. All from me. Spelling tests, report cards, school projects made out of magazine clippings, book reports. In the bottom of the box are my early works. Crayon scribblings. Stick figures. And the picture I was searching for. A drawing of a garden. Flowers, in rainbow colors. Our secret.

I leave the picture out and replace the box on the shelf.

In the back of the closet, behind my father's golf clubs, I find an empty gold frame. I slide the picture inside the frame and take it to my room. Then I go to the garage for a hammer and nail.

I hang the picture next to my bed. Where I can see it every morning when I open my eyes. I lie down on my bed and look at the picture. I can still feel Lizzie's hand around mine, guiding me.

I must fall asleep, because when I open my eyes again, it's dark outside.

Ethel is in the kitchen. She's making me her "famous" mac and cheese. And is it ever good. If Ethel realizes I've spent the afternoon in bed, she doesn't say anything about it. At dinner, she doesn't talk about anything serious. Instead, she decides we're going to play a game while we eat. We each have to make up funny reality-show ideas. Her best is *So You Think You Can Be a Clown*. My best is *American Mouse*.

After dinner, I decide to show Ethel some of my photographs. I don't show her the ones of Lizzie.

"They're real good. You've got a gift." Ethel laughs at one of Kona leaping in the air, her paws going every which way. "I like this one the best." Then she hands the pictures back to me. She rubs her chin. "Looking at these pictures gets me to thinking. Would you like a job?"

A job. I had planned on getting a job this summer. *Before*. I would like to make some extra money, though. My allowance is definitely not going to support photo paper and colored ink for long.

"What kind of job?" I ask her.

"I have this hobby—well, it's turned into more than

just a hobby. It's sort of a passion of mine, growing roses," Ethel begins. "I'm entered in the fall competition for the President's Trophy. So I'm gearing up for it. And I'd like to have some pictures of my babies. Some real good pictures. I think you could take them. And I'd pay you."

"I'm not very experienced," I tell her. "I don't even know how to use all the buttons on my camera."

"But you've got a good eye. And that's all that matters," Ethel assures me. "Anyway, you'll take better pictures than me, that's for sure."

I think about it. How hard could it be to shoot some flowers?

"Okay," I tell Ethel. "You just hired yourself a photographer."

"Do you want to start tomorrow?" she asks.

I nod and smile. It's not like I have anything else to do.

Chapter 12

The next day, bright and early, Ethel buckles me and Kona into her silver sedan and we zoom over to her house. I say "zoom" because Ethel drives fast. Very fast. Hold-on-to-your-hat fast. But at least Kona and I arrive in one piece, and Kona only throws up once.

Ethel's house is this little yellow cottage in an older, quiet neighborhood. The house is bordered by a white picket fence and the most gorgeous rosebushes you could ever imagine. And these aren't even the competition flowers. Those she keeps in a special area in her backyard.

They are all in separate containers. Ethel tries to explain it all to me, but after fifteen minutes on rose varieties, my eyes start to cross. It's like some kind of convoluted math equation.

The only thing I do need to understand is that Ethel has to produce one rose at each stage of bloom. One as a bud, one in opening bloom, and a third in full bloom. She has all these varieties with royal-sounding names like Lady Banks and Princess Grace. They are all different colors and each one of them is beautiful.

Ethel tells me to give her photographs of each and every flower. She will pay me $100 for the shoot. We shake on the deal and I get to work. Kona plays around on the grass while I adjust the pots to capture the best of the morning light. I shoot a few frames to test the color. Then I choose my first flower. It is a sunshine-yellow rose. I know Ethel called it a Lady Banks, but secretly, I call it Queen Lizzie. The color of the rose reminds me of the feeling I used to have when Lizzie would smile at me. The petals bend outward as if extending an offer of friendship. I step in to fill the entire frame with the flower. The autofocus tries to do its job, but something isn't right. I back up and then refocus. This time the beep sounds to let me know the picture is in focus. Only now I see the ground behind the flower. I try to stay where I am and zoom the lens in on the subject. This time when it beeps, I have the entire flower in frame and in focus. I click the button to capture the shot. I shoot a few more frames, just to be sure I have it.

I turn to a fully opened ruby rose. The petals are so rich and velvety that I have an overwhelming urge to touch them, to see if they feel as soft as they look. But I remember my mother telling me once that if you touch the petals of a flower, it can die. I certainly don't want to hurt any of Ethel's prizewinning flowers. The crimson color of the petals deepens at the edges where the petals ruffle up and turn dark maroon. It is captivating. I bend so that I come in just above and to the left of the rose. That way, I will capture how each petal lies back, revealing an amber-colored center.

My next subject is a pristine bud. It looks like it was supposed to be white, but at the last minute tricked Ethel as little veins of color trickled through the petals, turning the flower ever so slightly pink. The stem holds the bud aloft in a graceful arch. There is something in the way the solitary bud extends high that makes it seem independent—defiant. I try to translate this to the picture. I think I have the shot framed right, but I have a problem with the color of the rose. It is so pale, it comes out white in the first few

shots. I think maybe the brightness of the sunlight is wash-
ing it out. I move the pot. Resting fully in the shade, the
true color of the rose comes through.

After this, I choose a heavy sunset-colored rose laden
with petals, its lavender edges crinkling like a ribbon curling around a present just waiting to be opened. There is a
single drop of dew, shining like a jewel, hidden inside. The
petals hang sideways, so I have to lie down and rest my
elbows on the ground to keep the camera from moving. I
try to focus, but the camera is not still. I take a deep breath
and hold it in, willing my body to be still long enough to
get the image. I click the button and hope for the best. I've
always known roses were complicated flowers. But I had
no idea *how* complicated.

It is late afternoon when the sound of a lawn mower
breaks the silence and interrupts the solitude of my work.
I glance over the fence and am surprised to see none other
than Hunter Baxley mowing the lawn. My first instinct is
to duck. But he's already turned off the mower, and he's
walking toward me. I consider my options:

1. Run.
2. Hide.
3. Say hello.

The first two, while most appealing, should probably only be used in situations where the boy has not already spotted you. Which leaves me with option three. I force my feet to stay put and inwardly practice saying hi.

Hunter walks right up to the fence and we talk over the top of it.

"Hey, Jane," Hunter begins.

Okay, he knows my name. Which is surprising given that he only started school midyear and we've only had actual contact one time. One very embarrassing time. I know he moved here from somewhere in the Midwest and was instantly popular, which is impressive to me, since I've been at school with all the same kids since kindergarten and only managed to have two friends.

I realize he's staring at me. So I answer. "Hi."

"I've never seen you here before," Hunter says with a wide smile. I notice that he has matching dimples in both cheeks.

"No, I haven't been here before. I'm helping a friend," I say. I hold up my camera. "I'm taking pictures for her." Okay, so it's a partial truth. But do I really have to tell him that she's my babysitter?

"This is my grandparents' house," Hunter explains. "I live with them."

He's so open, I almost feel guilty for being secretive about Ethel. "I didn't know you lived with your grandparents," I say lamely. Just then Kona wakes from her nap in the shade and comes running over to meet a new friend.

"This is Kona," I say. "My dad and I just got her."

Hunter reaches over the fence to pet Kona's head. "Hi, Kona," he says to her. She licks his hand.

"So what kind of pictures are you taking?" he asks me.

"Flowers," I stammer. I wish I could just act normal. "Roses."

"Cool."

I nod and smile. I'm surprised to find that Hunter is friendly. In fact, he seems really nice.

"I'm really sorry about your sister," Hunter offers.

"Thank you," I say automatically. I look down at my shoes.

"I know how it feels," Hunter shares. "My parents were killed in a car accident. Eight months ago yesterday."

I'm shocked. So that explains why he moved in the middle of the school year. "I'm so sorry."

We stare at each other for a moment. Neither of us speaks. Our eyes just lock. And we understand each other.

Then Hunter breaks the silence. "Well, I better get back to mowing."

"Yeah, me, too. Well, not mowing . . . flowers," I stammer.

"Maybe I'll see you later."

"Sure," I respond. And I return to the roses.

But I don't see him later. I am lost in the beauty and art of my work. The slope of a pale lavender petal, the curve of a silky closed bud, the hopefulness of an open bloom reaching up to the sun mesmerize me. I work until dusk. And then Ethel takes me home.

We eat fried chicken and mashed potatoes for dinner.

"I never knew there were so many names for roses," I confess to Ethel. "Or that each one could look so different. They almost have personalities. And they smell so good."

She smiles at me. And then in a singsongy voice recites:

"What's in a name? that which we call a rose

By any other name would smell as sweet."

She pauses for dramatic effect. Then, "Mr. William Shakespeare. *Romeo and Juliet*. I know it doesn't sound all fancy the way I say it," Ethel admits. "But the meaning is the same. He's telling us that roses smell heavenly, no matter what we call them."

Then Ethel teaches me about floriography, the language of flowers.

"All flowers have a meaning," she explains. "It was mostly used during Victorian times," she explains. "If a gentleman sent a lady a red rose, she knew he was saying he loved her."

I'm fascinated. I want to know more. "What about other colors?" I ask.

"A white rose stands for innocence and friendship. Light pink for admiration and sympathy. Yellow with red tips, falling in love. Violet, love at first sight. Red and white together meant unity. And orange—*passion*." She says this last word like it's her favorite one in the English language. She draws out the sounds of the letters as if tasting each on her tongue.

I take all of this in. It's incredibly romantic. To think of people choosing the color of rose for someone to give them a secret message. Then I realize she hasn't mentioned the color of my Queen Lizzie rose.

"What about yellow?" I ask.

"Dying love," she answers. Her voice echoes in my head. I hear her words over and over. "Dying love, dying love, dying love."

I meet her eyes with mine. We are silent then. She knows. I know she can't possibly hear my innermost thoughts. Yet,

somehow, this woman I barely know understands. And so
she says nothing more. But it doesn't feel like the silence
when my parents and I were all thinking about Lizzie, but
not talking about our feelings. This silence feels comforting. As though we are remembering her and honoring her
silently. It's different. Peaceful. And pure.

That night, I am uploading all of today's photographs when
Dad calls. He tells me his trip has been extended for two
more days. I assure him that I'm okay and that I'm taking
good care of Kona, and Ethel is taking good care of me.
I admit to him that he was right, and it is good to have
someone here with me.

   After we hang up, I decide to call my mom. I've been
avoiding her calls for the last two days. But after talking
to Hunter today, I feel lucky to have both of my parents. I
want to hear my mother's voice.

   She's really happy to hear from me. She tells me she
misses me. I think she really means it. She asks me again
if I want to come to Sun City. She is worried about me
home alone. I tell her that I'm not alone, I have Ethel—
and Kona. There is a silent moment on the phone then. I
tell her I love her and then I hang up and go to sleep.

🌹

I wake up from a nightmare. Sweaty and tired. It's just before sunrise. No one is awake but me and the birds. I can hear them singing outside my window. Kona is curled into a little ball on the pillow next to mine. I've dispensed with Dad's crating system. Kona likes it better in my bed.

I'm afraid to go back to sleep, so I sit cross-legged on the floor and try some yoga breathing.

Breathe in peace, breathe out anger. Breathe in love, breathe out fear. I stretch forward and lay my head on the floor. Then I stand and lean forward for downward dog. I stay like that as long as I can, then I bend into child's pose. And up again into downward dog. All the time, I remind myself to breathe in, breathe out. I finish by lying on my back on the floor and closing my eyes. I focus on the light between my eyes. And I let my mind drift. I imagine a flock of white birds lifting the gray weight of a boulder from my shoulders. Ropes attached to the feet of the birds wrap around the boulder. The birds fly away. Taking my boulder with them. Over the horizon. Away from me.

I open my eyes and breathe in. I feel different. Rested. And maybe even a little bit peaceful. I stand and head for the computer. I click on the folder of Ethel's photos and I'm excited all over again to see each one appear on the screen. Looking at my work close up, I have to admit I've done a really good job. The roses are breathtaking. Each one is more beautiful than the last. And each stage of bloom is different. By the time I print them out, Ethel is calling me for breakfast. She has made waffles with whipped-cream happy faces and cherry noses.

Ethel loves the photographs. She compliments each one, pointing out the way I captured the dew on the petals or the simplicity of the blossom. I tell her I have at least one more day of work before I get all of the flowers. We plan to go over to her house again today. After breakfast, I go back upstairs and get dressed. Today, I don't feel like wearing my old cutoffs and blue T-shirt. I want to wear something special. I open my drawers. The trouble is, all I have are shorts and T-shirts, soccer uniforms, one going-to-church dress, one pirate costume, and the funeral dress.

But I know where I can find something fabulous to wear.

Lizzie's room is dark. The shutters are closed. I open them and light floods into the room. I pull open the closet doors and scan my choices. Floral dresses, gypsy skirts, and countless pairs of jeans stare back at me. I pull out some of the jeans and shimmy out of my sweats. I choose one pair of strategically faded low-rise jeans with flap pockets on the rear. I don't really expect them to fit. So I am shocked when I look at myself in the mirror. Other than the fact that they are so long they drag on the ground, I have to admit that they fit perfectly.

Then I choose a loose white gauze peasant top with embroidered red and blue flowers.

I decide to leave the shutters open as I cross through the bathroom and into my own room. I take a pen and my red-handled scissors out of my desk drawer and mark a spot on the jeans with the pen before I slip them off, laying them on the floor. With my scissors, I trim the jeans to a midcalf length. I put them back on, pull on the top, and twist my hair into a knot on top of my head. I check myself out in the mirror and I have to smile at myself.

Ethel notices right away. And unlike my parents, who might notice something but never comment, Ethel doesn't believe in hiding thoughts and feelings.

She places her hands on her hips. A wide grin spreads across her face.

"I should be taking pictures of *you*," she announces. "You're blooming."

chapter 13

I work all morning without seeing Hunter. Then, just before lunch, I hear someone next door. I glance over, but I can't see anything. When I walk closer, I find Hunter painting the fence.

"Hi," I say. I suddenly feel embarrassed about my dressed up look. I hope he doesn't notice. But he does.

"You look nice," he tells me.

Now I'm really embarrassed. I have absolutely no idea what to say. I manage to mumble a thank you.

Just then, Ethel pokes her head out the door and calls

to me. "Jane, lunchtime. Come and take yourself a break."

Then she notices Hunter. "Oh, hi there, handsome," she greets him. "Your grandma feed you lunch yet?"

"No," he says.

Ethel waves her hand in a big open gesture. "Well, come on and join us, then." Her smile is so inviting and her manner so confident. I want to be like her. I smile, too. At Hunter.

"Okay, thanks," he says, suddenly shy.

Hunter comes around the fence and is attacked by Kona's tongue. He laughs and picks her up. "I haven't had a dog since I was a little kid," he shares.

"My dad got her for me. I think he thought it would help," I tell him honestly. It's weird, but I don't feel any need to hide things with Hunter. I guess maybe it's because I know he just gets it.

He nods at me. "Even if it doesn't. It's still cool to have a dog."

I nod back. He's right, I realize. Even if Kona can't make missing Lizzie any easier. I do have a dog. And I have wanted one forever.

"Life's little blessings," Ethel adds as we follow her to the sunporch. She lays out another place for Hunter and then we all munch peanut-butter-and-jelly sandwiches, grapes, and snickerdoodle cookies. Ethel tells us funny stories about modeling and I tell a few about soccer matches. Hunter listens. And laughs. He doesn't share much with us.

After we clear the table, Ethel asks Hunter if he'd like to see some of the photos I've been shooting. When he says yes, she brings out the ones I printed that morning and lays them out all over the table. Normally, this would embarrass me immensely, but for some reason, I am okay with sharing the photos with Hunter.

"These are amazing." When he praises me, I think I must glow from the inside out.

"Did you do these in Photoshop?" he asks.

"I'm just learning," I admit.

"I could make some adjustments on my computer. If you want."

Ethel claps her hands. "Wonderful!"

So I spend the afternoon with Hunter Baxley, sitting next to him at his desk, while he edits my photographs. He teaches me how to work magic in Photoshop, and I absorb every word he says. He teaches me how to crop the photos, how to brighten the colors, and even how to remove something from the photo—like a leaf or a thorn.

Late in the afternoon, we sit cross-legged and facing each other in an old tree house Hunter's dad built when he was a little boy. It smells dusty, but it's cool and quiet inside. We toss a tennis ball back and forth. Hunter tells me about the night his parents died.

"They were on their way home from a holiday party. It was snowing. The roads were icy and stuff. They say Dad had too much to drink, that he shouldn't have been behind the wheel . . ."

His voice trails off. I don't speak. I imagine his parents on the icy road. Hunter at home, waiting for them.

"Anyway, it happened really fast. And neither of them even made it to the hospital."

I feel the wetness on my cheeks before I realize I am crying. He leans forward and gently brushes away my tears with his fingertips. Our eyes meet. For a moment, we stay like that. Without speaking. It's a silent moment. A moment of understanding. Of shared pain. A moment of the deepest connection.

Then he speaks, almost in a whisper. Haltingly. "I've never talked about it before."

I understand.

After dinner, I e-mail Zoe. And tell her about the photo job and seeing Hunter. I don't tell her about his parents. Some things are meant to be private. I know she's my best friend, but it's wrong to expose something so personal and painful that is someone else's to share when they're ready.

I'm just sending my e-mail when Ethel comes into my room carrying a vase of white roses.

She sets the vase on my desk. "This is for you," she says. "They reminded me of your family. Out of one stem, four white blossoms." I see what she means. All four roses are growing from one stem. The largest is pure white, in full bloom. Ethel points to it.

"That there's your dad." Then she points to the second largest rose. It is a bud halfway opened with some pink running through the petals. "And this one's your mama.

"That's you, Jane." Ethel indicates a tight bud with pink all around the outer petals and white on the inner petals. It is just beginning to flutter open on the edges. "Just beginning to bloom."

There is only one rose left. It's a bloom in the early stages of opening, but it has already begun to die. The edges of the white rose have turned to parchment. It is frozen forever midbloom.

I touch the rose gently. No fear of killing *this* flower. "*Lizzie,*" I whisper.

Ethel nods. I reach out and wrap my arms around her generous frame. She smells like vanilla and whipped cream. My eyes fill with tears.

"I miss my sister."

She holds me tight. "I know you do."

For some reason, it's easier to cry with Ethel than it was to cry with Zoe, my best friend. She just lets me cry. Eventually, she draws back and tilts my chin up so that I can look her in the eye. I'm not embarrassed about the wetness on my cheeks.

"Sisters are God's greatest gift," she tells me. "They know your strengths and your weaknesses. Your secrets and your fears. And even when it's their time to depart from this earth, no one will ever take their place in your heart and in your memories. Lizzie will always be with you, darling."

She taps my chest lightly. "In here. You remember that."

I nod. Ethel wipes away a few of her own tears. "Now, I think I owe you some money."

I love the way Ethel can have a really deep moment with you one minute and then put on a cheerful face the next. It makes everything seem like it's going to be okay.

She takes a folded bill out of her pocket and hands it to me.

"Congratulations on a job well done," she says.

I unfold the money and find a hundred-dollar bill in my hand. I look at the picture of Ben Franklin in awe. I just earned my first money as a photographer—and I loved every minute of it. That night, I go to sleep with a smile on my face.

Dad arrives home the next day. He's brought me a red T-shirt with white writing that reads SAN FRANCISCO. It's a total airport gift, but I don't tease him about it. Actually, I'm really happy to see him. But I know that Dad coming home means Ethel is leaving. I have to admit I am sad. But I'm also thrilled to have my freedom back.

Ethel hugs me tight and tells me to keep my chin up. I nod and try not to cry.

"You are a brave girl, Jane," Ethel tells me. "Thank you for letting me share some of your summer. You let a lonely woman have a family for a few days."

I listen to her words, and I can't believe Ethel is thanking me. I never thought about her life being lonely, or that she might have enjoyed our time together. I just thought about how it made me feel.

I wave good-bye at the door. I know I will be seeing her soon. But the house feels sad and lonely again once she's gone.

Dad sits down at the table to eat, and I bring him a stack of my photographs. He takes his time and looks through every one. He's really impressed.

"We're going to have to get you a portfolio to hold all your work," he tells me.

I tell him about Hunter teaching me how to use Photoshop. I try not to gush about Hunter and give away my feelings. Not that I have feelings for Hunter. I just like him, is all. But no one wants their dad to know what boys they like or don't like. I think Dad sees through me anyway because he raises an eyebrow and gets a kind of I-know-something-that-you-don't-want-me-to-know smirk around the corners of his mouth, but says nothing.

I wonder why Dad and I are getting along so much better now than we used to. Maybe because it's just the two of us now, I think. Like people stranded. Dad and I are the only ones left. We only have each other.

And then a teeny, tiny thought creeps in. A putrid-green thought. It's very, very small, but it won't be ignored.

Maybe, just maybe now, with Lizzie gone, Dad has to see me, Jane.

It's the kind of thought you want to pretend you never have and it makes me feel guilty, for being so selfish. And for being jealous of a ghost.

I think of Lizzie and what she would say about this if I confessed it to her. If I shared my innermost feelings. The answer comes to me instantly, as though I can hear her speaking. She tells me that it's okay. For once, I'm the one who needs to hear that. And it *is* okay. Because no matter how it's happened, my life has changed, and there's absolutely nothing I can do about it. Whether I like it or not, I am no longer invisible.

Chapter 14

The afternoon belongs to me. Dad heads off to run errands, and I am free to do anything I want. I kick around a soccer ball in the front yard. I have just started teaching Kona how to play the game when Hunter rides up on his bike.

"Hi," I say, surprised to see him.

"Hi," he says back.

I think I am blushing. I know I am beaming. I don't say anything else right away. I'm just happy to see him.

"Did you ride your bike all the way over here?" I ask. "That's really far."

Now *he's* embarrassed. He looks down at his sneakers. His left hand brushes back his chin-length hair. I notice that the ends are slightly lighter in color, like the tip of a paintbrush. I wish I could touch it. Then I realize he's caught me staring at his hair. I feel even my pinkie toes turn red as I quickly look away.

"Are you practicing?" he asks.

I can't believe he would ride all this way just to see me. I wonder if he has something he needs to talk about.

"No, just teaching Kona a few tricks. You wanna kick the ball around with us?"

Hunter smiles then. He starts to look more at ease. "Sure."

We kick the ball back and forth, and Kona chases after it. Before long, all the awkwardness has disappeared.

When we get hot, I grab some Popsicles from the freezer, and we both sit sideways across the hammock in the backyard. We let our feet dangle and we take turns pushing off the ground to keep us swinging back and forth. I lift Kona onto the hammock and she lies between us.

"Do you believe in heaven?" I ask Hunter.

"I think so," he answers. "My parents talk to me in my dreams. And sometimes when I wake up, I feel like they've been there. Do you think that's weird?"

I shake my head no. "I wear Lizzie's clothes sometimes. And most nights I sleep in her bed," I confess.

"Do you think she wanted to die?" Hunter asks me.

If anyone else had asked me this, I would scream and yell at them and defend my sister's honor and reputation. But with him, it's different.

"I don't know," I say honestly. "I want to believe it was an accident."

Hunter nods. He doesn't speak. We push—back and forth, back and forth—both lost in our own thoughts.

"Do you blame your dad for what happened?" I ask Hunter.

His eyes widen slightly, and I see his face tense around the mouth. I suddenly wish I had thought about what I was going to say before I let the words out of my mouth. But it's too late. Hunter looks down at his hands. He reaches out and strokes Kona around the ears. I don't speak. I don't even breathe. I think I've made a big mistake and now maybe he doesn't want to be my friend anymore.

"It's like what you just said about your sister. I want to believe it wasn't his fault."

I know how that feels. There's this part of me that tells myself Lizzie didn't want to die, that she didn't hurt herself on purpose. But there's another part of me that knows that's a lie.

"But I hate him sometimes. For what he did to me. And my mom."

My heart aches for him. "I know how that feels," I tell him honestly. "It's this secret bad feeling that you have—but you can't tell anyone about it because we're not supposed to be angry."

Hunter nods. His eyes look large in his face. "Ethel would say that some things just can't be helped," I finish.

"I like Ethel," Hunter announces.

"Me, too," I agree.

"Do you think you'll ever forgive your dad?" I ask. I'm not sure if I'm really asking Hunter this question, or if I'm asking myself.

He shrugs. "Does it matter?"

I think it does matter. I think if we can't forgive, we can never be free. "I think so," I tell him honestly.

"I don't know," is his answer. And the truth is, it's mine as well.

We're silent then. All I can hear are the birds chirping in the trees, Kona breathing, the creaking of the hammock. I finish my Popsicle and resist the urge to chew on the stick. I'm certain Lizzie never would have chewed on a Popsicle stick in front of a boy.

I have to say something that's been on my mind. I take a deep breath. "I'm sorry I was rude that day under the bleachers. I just didn't want anyone to see me like that."

"I just wanted you to know you weren't alone."

"Thank you," I tell him. Our eyes meet for a long moment. We say nothing, but just stare at each other. Then Hunter breaks the silence.

"You know what you should do?" he says suddenly, his eyes twinkling. "You should make a memory box."

"What's that?" I ask.

Hunter sits up and faces me. "You take a box. A shoe box, wooden box, anything really. And you put things in it that remind you of the person you lost. Photos, ticket stubs from a movie you went to together, a T-shirt, their favorite book. And then you put it in a place you can find it whenever you need it. I have mine underneath my bed."

"That's a great idea," I tell him. I love the thought of this. I thank him for sharing it with me.

"I'm really glad you came over to Ethel's to take pictures," Hunter blurts out. "I always wanted to talk to you at school. But you always seemed so busy with your friends."

I think this is incredibly ironic. That Mr. Popular thought I was too busy.

Just then, Hunter leans over and presses his lips against

mine. I have no idea what to do, so I press mine against his. Electricity shoots through my body, from my lips to my toes and back again. Hunter pulls away and looks at me with his chocolate eyes. I melt.

And it dawns on me.

I just had my first kiss.

And my very next thought: *I wish I could tell Lizzie.*

"I want to show you something," I tell him. I jump off the hammock and run upstairs. I am breathing heavily as I pull out the photos of Lizzie lying in her coffin. I gather them tightly to my chest and take them back outside.

I hand the photos to Hunter.

He looks at them one by one. I see them again, as if for the first time. Lizzie's hands. So white and still. Folded in a serene way that is so un-Lizzie. Lizzie's mouth with the strings keeping her lips from opening. The coffin, like a prison enclosing her in white satin. The roses. Drooping heavy with the weight of their petals. She would have hated the pose they put her in, I think. It was so angelic. The type of pose that showed her the way people thought she was—or expected her to be—but wasn't really her at all.

Hunter finishes looking at all the photos.

"Do you think it's weird?" I ask him.

He shakes his head. "Not at all."

I exhale then. And I realize that I have been so worried about myself. I thought I was losing my mind. Hunter telling me that it's okay makes me feel better. I smile at him as I take the pictures from his hands.

"She called me J," I tell him. "No one else ever called me that."

Hunter considers this for a long moment. "Would you want someone else to call you J?"

"I don't think so," I admit. I think I want that nickname to forever remind me of Lizzie. Even though I still feel the heavy rock of missing her pressing down in the middle of my chest, thinking of Lizzie calling me J spreads like warm lava flowing over the rock. I want to hold on to that feeling.

Hunter leaves a little while later. He doesn't say anything, but he gives me one of those deep, soul-searching looks that makes my stomach do flip-flops. I lean over and give him a soft kiss on the cheek. His hair softly brushes against my lips. It smells like oranges and salt. I pull back and see him smiling at me. He pushes a strand of loose hair off my cheek.

"I'll send you an e-mail later," he promises.

"Okay," I manage. I can barely breathe.

I watch him ride off. Then I go inside to make some dinner for Dad and me. When Mom was home, I hated cooking. But Ethel made cooking fun. And now I like it.

I make Ethel's "famous" mac and cheese. Dad loves it. We laugh and talk at dinner. There are only two places now.

"Guess what?" Dad teases over our dessert of ice-cream sundaes.

"We're getting a horse?"

Dad snorts. "That's funny, Jane. No, I finally booked a trip for us."

"Where?" I ask, afraid to hear the answer. Some of Dad's travel ideas are a bit on the outlandish side.

"Santa Barbara," he responds. "And Kona is coming with us."

Santa Barbara is close to where we drove to get Kona. It's only a couple of hours away. And it's beautiful. Wide beaches, lots of sunshine, volleyball nets on the sand.

"For ten days, you and I are going to splash in the surf, lie on the beach, and read books, snorkel, and sightsee," Dad promises.

A Holden family vacation finally comes to fruition. But with only half of the Holden family.

A couple of weeks ago, I wouldn't have been able to go on a vacation. But I'm beginning to understand that life takes you forward, even when you don't want to go. You can stay in your pajamas, hide in your bedroom, and cry until you have no more tears. But still, life will push you onward.

Tomorrow, life is taking me to Santa Barbara.

Chapter 15

Santa Barbara. The only word to describe it is glorious. The deep blue ocean stretches out to the horizon as if racing with the sky. The beach is warm and breezy at the same time. Lively but quiet, it is the perfect place for a vacation.

Dad and I have a hotel room across the street from the beach. We wake up in the morning and pack up snacks, sunblock, and books. For Dad, it's science fiction; mysteries for me. We rent lounge chairs and umbrellas and sit back and relax. Although Kona doesn't let us sit for long because she wants to chase seagulls or splash in the waves. Dad and I take long walks along the shore. Sometimes we point out funny things along the way, and sometimes we are just quiet.

In the afternoons, when people start packing up and the beach starts looking empty, that's when I think about Lizzie. I sink my feet into the still-warm sand, and I wonder where she is now.

Maybe heaven is a place where souls congregate and float around. Or maybe it's a place of resting until the soul comes back to earth in another body. I wonder if Lizzie is watching me from up above. If she can hear my thoughts and read my mind. If she can help me understand why she had to leave us. I think of all the bad people in the world who are alive, and I don't think it's fair. And I think a lot about what I could have done differently. How I could have helped Lizzie so this would never have happened. If I had listened better or stood up for her more, maybe she would still be here. Then I wonder if she were still here, if things would be like this anyway, with our family torn apart. The thoughts drift through my mind like a balloon floating across the sky. Would Lizzie and I have visited Hawaii together? Did she know how much I loved her? Will I ever see her again?

And when I can't take it a second longer, I think about Lizzie's favorite moment. Because after a great deal of contemplation, I have finally decided that heaven is a place where you get to be in your favorite moment for eternity. So I think of what Lizzie would choose. The thing she would most like to relive over and over if she could. I think it would be the day I came home from the hospital, when my mother first laid me in her arms and told her I was her new baby sister. Lizzie had a picture of that day in a frame in her room. And she always told me that she believed I was hers and no one else's. I know that was her favorite moment. And I know that she loved me more than anyone.

I watch the waves roll in and out. I think about what I would say to Lizzie if she could hear me now. I would tell her that I'm sorry. Sorry for being jealous of her. Sorry for not taking good enough care of her. Sorry for thinking she was perfect. And I would make her a promise. That I would always be true to myself. And never try to be anyone but me. I think she would be proud of me for that.

We call Mom every night. And each time, she tells me how much she misses me and wishes she was with us. I'm not sure I can imagine her being here. I feel guilty thinking that if she were on this vacation, it would spoil everything.

❧

One afternoon, Dad asks me if I want to go to the Santa Barbara Zoo. I think it sounds fun, so I pack up my camera and we head off.

Dad wants to start with the reptile house. It is so dark inside that I don't bother trying to take any pictures.

"I wish your mother could see this," Dad says as he looks at a twenty-foot boa constrictor. Mom is terrified of snakes, so this makes both of us laugh. Then he places his arm around my shoulder. "What do you say we go feed some birds?"

Dad and I push open the wooden door and step through a plastic curtain to find ourselves in the lorikeet exhibit. Here, we purchase little paper cups full of nectar. We are supposed to hold the cups out and wait for the little birds to come by and sip from the cups.

"Lorikeets are parrots that love to drink nectar," the attendant tells us. "If you hold really still with your arm outstretched, they will sit on your hand to drink."

I do exactly as the lady tells me, and I wait. After a few minutes, a bird alights on my wrist and begins sipping from the cup. The bird is small, about the size of my hand. And it is absolutely gorgeous. It has a bright reddish beak with a blue face and a yellow head. A green patch covers its back, and underneath, it has an orange breast. While I am admiring the bird on my hand, Dad is admiring one of his own. Or rather, the bird is admiring Dad. For as I look to my left, I see that there is a lorikeet perched on top of Dad's head. Another is sitting on his arm and yet a third is on his shoulder.

"I think you might need to stay at the zoo, Dad," I say. "The birds have mistaken you for a tree."

Dad laughs, and I shoot a photo of him with the birds.

Then we make our way up a small hill. We can see the ocean from the top. It stretches out to the horizon. The green grass is lush all around. It is so peaceful. The sound of birds chirping mixes with monkey calls and the laughter of children. Halfway up the hill, we see the giraffes. There is a small platform set up next to the exhibit and people are waiting in line to feed them.

"Would you like to try?" Dad asks. I nod yes.

It only takes a few minutes before we're at the front of the line. The zoo attendant lets us step onto the platform.

"Giraffes are the tallest living land mammals," she begins. "They are herbivores, which means that they eat plants. And giraffes love to eat. They will spend up to twenty hours a day eating."

As she speaks, the herd of giraffes draws closer to the platform.

"They know it's snack time," she tells us.

One of the animals has a crooked neck. Its head is bent over to the side.

"Is that one injured?" Dad asks.

"No," the attendant informs us. "She developed a kink in her neck. But she is able to live a normal life. We watch over her to make sure that she isn't in pain or having any problems. She's been happy here for twenty years now."

Then she tells us not to make any sudden movements because we could scare the giraffes. She also tells us not to turn our backs to them. And to beware of kisses. Next, she places a small biscuit in my hand. A giraffe leans over the fence. We are raised high on this platform so that the giraffe can look us right in the eye. The giraffe leans close and suddenly this impossibly long black tongue swipes out of her mouth and completely slimes my hand. Somewhere in the process, the giraffe manages to take the biscuit. And I am left with this icky goo all over my wrist.

"Yuck," I say to Dad. He just laughs. Then the giraffe leans in and swipes my cheek with her tongue.

"She likes you," the attendant informs me.

Yippee for me. I wipe my cheek with the back of my hand. I feed two more giraffes. One of them, the one with the crooked neck. She is very sweet, though she drools from the side of her mouth. Then I step back and take a few photos. I get one of the giraffe close up, her warm brown eyes gently begging for more treats. And I capture one of the biggest giraffe swiping Dad's hair with her tongue.

We see more animals nearby. A baby anteater perches on the top of her mother's back, their stripes matching up so that the baby blends into the mother's coat. A snow leopard dozes in the afternoon sun. A red panda chases its tail. And two Channel Island foxes play tag. I shoot photos of all of them. And Dad and I have a terrific time together.

After that, we leave the zoo and walk back to our hotel. On the way, we stop and look at the artist booths set up along the boardwalk. There are original paintings, sculptures, jewelry, even handmade toys. At one booth, there are silver cuff bracelets with engraved flowers on them. There are all different flowers to choose from—daisies, tulips, orchids, and of course roses. Dad asks me if I like them.

I nod and tell him that I do like them, very much. Dad picks up the rose bracelet and slips it on my wrist. He pays the man for the bracelet.

"To remind you of your first professional photo shoot," Dad says.

"And our trip," I add as I give him a hug.

Dad picks out a watercolor silk scarf for Mom. And we also buy three hand-painted purple-and-yellow butterflies to hang in my room.

I send Hunter ten postcards—one for each day we're away. I choose the most beautiful pictures I can find. Sunsets, waves, whales leaping over the ocean. On one of them, I even get brave enough to write *Miss you*. I think this is a really big step for me. Hunter sends me a few e-mails. In one of them, he tells me he misses me, too. At the end, he writes *Love, H*. I read this part over and over.

On our last day in Santa Barbara, Dad and I decide to go whale watching. First thing in the morning, we rent bikes from the hotel and ride over to the pier.

We board the whale watching boat with the other tourists and sit side by side against the railing. I enjoy the bobbing motion of the ship as it navigates through the choppy water. The wind blows my hair around my face and it stings my eyes. My skin feels cool where the air touches and almost raw. There is no way Dad and I can talk over the wind and the sound of the ship's motor, so we just smile at each other and point to things.

I notice that Dad looks a little green. I'm reminded of a

time he got seasick on a boat trip to Catalina Island. I wonder if he's feeling a little queasy now. Just then, he grabs my elbow and points to the right side of the ship. There, not ten feet away from us, is a pod of dolphins. I can see their silvery backs as they rise out of the waves to swim alongside the boat. I quickly lift my camera from around my neck and pull off the lens cap. I start shooting. Suddenly one breaks the water and leaps into the air. I catch it midleap, its body arching gracefully through the air. It is breathtaking. I turn to Dad and smile. Dad grins back. A few minutes later, we circle a buoy covered with an entire herd of seals sunbathing. It makes me laugh. I shoot a few photos. One actually lifts his head and looks my way. I capture his lazy eyes looking at me, his whiskers twitching just slightly.

We don't spot any whales. But we don't mind. When we return to shore, we walk on the pier, and Dad buys me an ice cream. I get chocolate chip in a waffle cone. Dad decides to stick with a soda. He confesses to me that he feels a little nauseated. I resist the urge to tease him about it. Nothing feels worse than being sick and having someone laugh at you. And anyway, I think he knew he'd get sick, but he went anyway, just for me. And when someone does something like that for you, it feels really good. I don't want to joke that feeling away. I want to enjoy it.

I lick my ice cream as we watch fishermen hauling in their catches. Then I lean over the railing and look down at the water so far below. Dad and I have avoided talking about anything serious for the entire vacation. But now that we're about to go home, I want to know what to expect.

"Are you and Mom getting a divorce?" I pose the question to him gently. I am afraid to hear a yes and equally afraid to hear a no.

"What makes you think that?" Dad asks.

I shrug. "She's been gone almost the whole summer."

"She needed a break," he answers.

This irks me beyond belief. "From what, Dad?" I ask. "From me, from you, from her life?"

Dad puts his arm around me and squeezes me tightly. "This is about your mother, Jane. Not about you," he assures me. "You haven't done anything wrong."

"Then why does she hate me?" I ask.

He has no answer for this. He takes a breath and looks out at the ocean.

"Jane, your mother doesn't hate you. She loves you."

"But she loved Lizzie more," I say softly, the tears stinging my eyes. Saying it out loud hurts deep inside my heart. So much, it feels like it will break apart into little pieces.

"Oh, Jane," he says. "It's not about loving one of you more than the other. Your mother loves you both. So do I. But Lizzie was so much like your mother. She was just bonded to her differently than she is to you. It's not better or worse. It's just different."

I study his eyes. I believe he is telling me the truth, but I want him to know how it feels to be me. How it feels to be the forgotten one.

"My whole life, I've felt like I was compared to Lizzie. She was there first. And she was perfect. I could never measure up. I feel so bad saying this, because I loved her more than anyone. But I did it, too. Everything was always about Lizzie. And even though she's not here anymore, it's still all about Lizzie."

Dad pulls me close, places his hands on the sides of my face. "Jane, you have always been you. Not anyone else. And I never expected you to be Lizzie. If I paid more attention to her, maybe it was because she needed it. You didn't. You have this strength of spirit that doesn't need constant filling up."

"Really?" I ask.

"Really," Dad answers. Then he brushes my hair off my face. "We both need to learn to make peace with the past."

"I know," I tell him. "But I just can't."

"Then it's too soon, Little Bunny. Trust yourself. I trust you."

Tears are streaming down my cheeks. I'm on the pier crying my eyes out in front of tourists and fishermen, but I don't care. I throw myself into my father's arms and hold on tight.

We drive home in the late afternoon, and I watch the sun set outside my window. The ocean turns pink and gold. Surfers ride the waves in to shore. Dogs run on the sand. Children splash in the water. I smile at Dad. And he smiles back. Kona crawls into the front seat and lies down in my lap. I am happy.

Chapter 16

The next morning, Mom comes home.

I'm in my room, working on the pictures from our trip, when I hear her voice calling me. Kona starts puppy barking.

"Jane, Jane. I'm home!"

"Quiet, sweetie. It's okay," I tell her. I remember that the last time Mom saw Kona she stormed out to the garage for a cigarette.

I don't rush downstairs to see her. I take my time and finish what I am doing first. After all, she has been gone almost the whole summer without a care. And I'm angry about it. That's the truth, and I'm not going to hide it.

I hear her open my door. Kona starts to bark again.

"Oh, there you are," she says. I turn and look at her. I am completely shocked.

She looks so different. Her face is all suntanned and her hair is loose and kind of wavy. She's wearing a gauzy orange tunic over jeans with some kind of amber-colored beads around her neck. And she is smiling. Really smiling. All the way to her eyes. She looks so much like Lizzie that it takes my breath away.

She holds out her arms to me. "I missed you."

I stand and reluctantly let her hug me. I am not sure who this is.

She squeezes me tight. Then she lets me go and looks me in the eye.

"You look pretty," she tells me. "More grown-up. I can tell you're starting seventh grade in a couple of weeks."

I am embarrassed. I don't know what to say. Then she sees the photos up on the computer screen.

"Oh, are these your photos?" she asks. "Your dad told me how you've been working on them all summer. He said you're very talented."

She peers at them. I curb the instinct to hit the button

and close the file. I don't want her looking at them. She has no right to just disappear for six weeks and then come back and act like Mother Earth.

"Jane, these are wonderful." She claps her hands together. A memory flashes into my mind of being little and coloring a picture of a red and orange sun. My mother praising me. I quickly push the image from my mind.

"I love the one of the giraffe."

She doesn't seem to notice that I am not speaking.

Then she does the thing that shocks me the most. She bends down and picks Kona up. She looks the puppy in the eye.

"I guess you and I are going to have to get to know each other, aren't we?" Kona licks her face. *Traitor.*

"Well, I'm going to unpack. Come in when you're done," she offers. I nod vaguely. I have absolutely no intention of going into her room to spend quality time with her.

A couple of hours later, Mom comes back into my room. I am sitting cross-legged on my floor with my eyes closed. *Breathe in. Breathe out. Breathe in. Breathe out.*

She waits for me to open my eyes. "I made you some lunch," she tells me.

"I'm not really hungry," I tell her, and close my eyes again. *Breathe,* I tell myself. *Breathe.*

I expect her to leave my room. But instead she sits down on the floor next to me. I sigh. *Who is this woman? And why won't she leave me alone?*

She waits there until I open my eyes again. Which I do. Because even though I am annoyed, she is my mother. And I know my father will be angry with me for disrespecting her.

"What?" I ask her, in an irritated voice.

"I want to explain everything to you. To tell you things, but I want to do it as a family." Her voice tightens a bit. I feel the pang as I am reminded aloud of Lizzie's absence. Even though I feel it all the time, every minute of every day, it hurts so much more to say anything about it aloud. Mom feels it, too; I can see her eyes tear up. But she keeps going.

"I want to talk to you and your father together. I can see you are angry with me and I understand. You have a right to be. Can you wait until tonight and at least hear me out?"

Now I really have no idea who this woman is. My mother never talks like this. Did aliens take over her body in the Arizona desert?

"I guess," I tell her. She smiles at me. Another real smile.

Then she completely changes the subject. "You were the most incredible baby," she tells me. "You were so independent. And so smart. You wanted to do everything yourself. You used to say, 'Me do it.'" She laughs. "It was so cute. You were the most adorable child I had ever seen. You used to make such messes. Into everything. One day you made mud pies, and the next you took apart the pantry. You were head-to-toe covered in flour. You already know that I named your sister after Elizabeth Bennet, the heroine of *Pride and Prejudice* and I named you Jane after her sister, Jane Bennet. But what you don't know is that by the time you were one year old, I decided I had made a terrible mistake. *You* were the one who embodied the spirit of the strong-willed, independent Lizzy Bennet, and your sister was more like sweet, compliant Jane."

She's right, this is the first time I have ever heard this. I know I've heard my mother talk for years about how she always wishes she could be like Elizabeth Bennet. So I think this is the biggest compliment she could give me.

Mom wraps her arms around her legs. "I was so used to everything being perfectly orderly. Everything in its place. And then you came along. I think God sent you to show me the things I had been missing in life. Because when you are trying to make everything perfect, you miss the spontaneity of life. That's you, Jane. The spark of life."

I don't say anything. I am trying to process all of it. I had always thought I was a disappointment after perfect Lizzie. I realize now that I've never had the same pressures as Lizzie. Lizzie carried them for me. And maybe the expectation of being perfect like Lizzie wasn't something my parents ever asked me to do, but was something I forced on myself. Before, I always thought this was because they thought I could never be that perfect, but now I understand that they've always seen me for who I am, but that I refused to see myself.

Mom pats my leg gently. Then she stands and is about to leave my room when she notices the crayon drawing on the wall.

"Oh, I remember this," she says as she steps closer to take a better look. "You and Lizzie drew this together. But she told us you had drawn it all by yourself. Your dad and I wanted to make sure you didn't feel like you were always in Lizzie's shadow. So we pretended to believe her. You were so proud of this picture." Mom touches the picture. She turns and smiles at me before she leaves.

It's only after she is gone that I realize: she doesn't smell like cigarettes anymore.

🌹

That night, when Dad comes home from work, we all sit down in the living room together. Mom wants to talk to us. I watch them together. To see if they look like people who are getting divorced. We give Mom her scarf. Mom opens it and smiles, then she kisses Dad lightly on the cheek. Not exactly a ringing endorsement for a happy marriage. But it isn't hostile either.

Dad and I sit side by side on the sofa. Mom sits across from us in one of the armchairs. She has changed into another gauzy tunic. Blue. With matching blue beads. Even when Mom goes bohemian, she's still matchy-matchy.

Despite all my breathing exercises, my stomach is in knots. I am so afraid my family is going to be broken into even tinier pieces tonight. *If they get divorced, who will I live with? Will I have to choose?* If Lizzie were here, we could have handled it together. But if Lizzie were still here, I think, maybe this wouldn't be happening. My palms are hot and my face feels frozen.

"I wanted to talk to you both together," Mom begins. She takes a deep breath.

Here it comes, I think. I prepare myself for the worst. And it is in that split second that I realize I love my family. I want us to stay together.

"First, I want to apologize. For running away. And leaving both of you here to fend for yourselves. It wasn't right of me to do that."

Mom looks directly at me. "And I can understand if you're resentful or angry. Because I would be, too."

Then she looks at Dad. "I needed some time to reflect on things. On me. And I couldn't do it here. Where . . ." Her voice suddenly falters. We know what she is trying not to say: where Lizzie killed herself. "That's why I tried to clean the room. It was just to help clear my head. I'm sorry if that upset you." She says this last part to me.

"I just wanted to tell you both that I am so sorry," she tells us. "It's all my fault." Her tears start to flow, and she is bawling. But she's not trying to hide it from me and Dad. She's out there in the open.

Dad reaches forward and envelops her in his arms immediately. He kisses her hair, the top of her head. "*Shhh, shhh,*" he is whispering to her. "We'd both change things if we could. To bring her back. It's not your fault. I'm sorry I said those things to you."

I start to cry. I have no idea what is going on.

Mom reaches out and grabs me tight. She brings me into their hug. Now I am mushed between them.

Finally, Mom lets go and brushes her tears away.

Dad takes Mom's face in his hands. Now he's crying. "I love you, Catherine. I thought I lost you, too." Then he kisses her.

I have never seen them kiss on the lips before. It freaks me out. I have to look away. But then I peek back. Just for a second. I have to admit that it does feel good to see your parents loving each other. Especially when you thought they were probably getting a divorce.

Then Mom places her hands on my shoulders. Her eyes are the deepest blue. "We are going to get through this. All of us."

I nod. "I love you," she tells me. I reach out and hug her. Tight. Probably tighter than I've ever hugged anybody in my life. And she hugs me back.

Then Dad hugs me. And I hug him back. And that's about all the touchiness the Holden family can handle.

"Anyone hungry?" Mom asks.

I don't know if we're hungry. But we all go in anyway. And we sit at the table. As a family. With three places instead of four. And even though we all notice, we try to come together and share our memories instead of pretending we feel nothing.

Chapter 17

Mom invites Ethel, Hunter, Hunter's grandparents, Zoe and Misty and their families over for an end-of-summer party. Mom buys me a new bathing suit for the occasion. It's an aqua one-piece with three straps across the back and sparkly flowers across the top. For once, I actually like sparkles.

I help Mom make her famous chili and corn bread. Dad decorates the yard with twinkle lights. Ethel brings chocolate cream pies. We go swimming and eat by the pool.

Ethel wears a purple bathing suit with an attached skirt. Complete with matching purple bathing cap. She dives in right away. So does Kona. For a Holden family gathering, it goes pretty well. We all chat and share stories about our summer vacations.

After she dries off, Ethel presents me with an invitation to her upcoming rose show.

"I was wondering if you would like to come as my photographer," she says. "I think there are some other folks there who might like you to take photos of their flowers. But none of 'em are as gorgeous as mine," she adds.

"Thank you," I tell her. "I'd love to come."

"And my neighbor Millie, across the street, would like to call you as well. She shows beagles. And she'd like to hire you to take pictures of her pooches."

I grin. I guess I have some experience shooting dogs.

I take photographs to remember the day. Mom laughing. Dee and Dum side by side eating corn on the cob. Kona shaking her wet fur. Zoe and Misty, heads close together, sharing secrets. Ethel in all her purple glory. Mom and Dad's hands, linked together. Hunter, looking at me.

After dinner, Hunter and I take Kona for a walk and I get my second kiss. It sends little butterflies dancing all over my stomach again. I can't stop smiling. Hunter holds my hand the whole way back to the house.

At the end of the night, I hand out red and white roses to everyone.

"These roses are a symbol of unity," I tell them. "I would now like to ask everyone to share in a moment of silence. In honor of Lizzie."

Everyone bows their heads like they are in prayer. Maybe some pray, maybe some think. I don't pray or think. Instead, I talk to Lizzie. In my heart. I tell her I miss her and that I wish she were here. And that I will never, ever forget her.

When the silence has ended, Dad tells me that he appreciates the idea so much that he thinks it should become a new Holden family tradition. Because even though we are all trying to be more open, it doesn't come naturally for us. Sharing a moment of silence for Lizzie every night gives us a way to connect with our grief. And to honor Lizzie at the same time.

Before she leaves, Ethel takes me aside and wraps me in one of her hugs. "You grab onto happiness with two hands, darling. Life's all about the journey. You remember that."

"I will, Ethel," I promise.

School starts the last week of August. Mom takes me shopping and I choose a new backpack, jeans, tank tops, sneakers, and a blue fisherman's cap. Mom takes me to get a haircut.

And as we leave the salon, she surprises me by taking me by the arm and leading me into a jewelry store down the street.

"What are we doing now?" I ask her.

"Getting your ears pierced," she announces. "I think this moment is long overdue."

I can't believe it. I really can't believe it. It's finally happening.

I'm getting my ears pierced.

The jewelry store is a vintage-looking shop decorated like the inside of a house. There are little sofas with flower prints on the cushions and the jewelry is laid out on wooden dressers. A girl with long black hair parted in the middle and a long white lacy shirt over rolled-up jeans introduces herself as Grace and asks us if we need any help.

"My daughter wants to get her ears pierced," my mother tells her—proud of me. It's a tone I remember hearing in her voice when she would speak about Lizzie, but never about me. It makes me feel warm right in the center of my chest.

"Okay. First you have to choose your earrings," Grace tells us. She takes out a box of earrings. There are all different birthstones to choose from—pearls, garnets, amethysts, aquamarines.

"The pink ones are pretty," Mom comments as she points to a pair of light pink earrings. "Those are usually only used for babies and little girls," Grace informs us.

That's enough for me to pass on the pink.

I decide on the cubic zirconias. They look like diamonds set in silver. I know they will go with everything.

Grace leads me to a high stool with a gingham pillow on it. I perch on the pillow and pretend not to be nervous. But the truth is, until this very moment, it never occurred to me that this might actually hurt.

"First I need to clean your ears," Grace says as she swipes at my earlobes with some cotton pads dipped in something that smells like rubbing alcohol.

Then she holds up a purple pen.

"I'm going to use this to mark the spots before I pierce them," she tells me.

I nod mutely. Grace hands me a small mirror framed in white wood. I hold it up and watch as she places tiny dots in the center of my earlobes.

"How does that look?" Grace asks.

I peer closely. It looks fine to me. I glance over at my mom. She nods her approval.

"I like it," I tell Grace.

Then I watch as Grace takes one of the earrings I selected out and slides it into the piercing gun.

I feel my stomach clench.

"It only pinches for a second," Grace says in a calming voice.

Babies do this, I remind myself as I grit my teeth. Grace positions the piercing gun on my ear. I feel my mother's hand slip gently around mine and hold on firmly.

"One, two," Grace counts.

On "three," I hold my breath and wait for the searing pain. It doesn't come. Just a little pinch.

"Done," Grace announces proudly, and moves around to do the other side.

Now I'm an old pro. The second one is done even faster than the first. Grace hands me the mirror.

There they are. Two shimmering earrings. In my ears!

I, Jane Holden, have pierced ears.

Then the flash runs through my mind, as fast as a shooting star across a navy-blue sky. I wish Lizzie was here to share this with me.

"They look beautiful," my mother compliments.

Hearing her voice brings me back to the moment. I throw my arms around her and squeeze as tight as I can.

Now I am ready to start seventh grade.

School starts on a Wednesday. Zoe, Misty, and I plan out what we are wearing for our first day. We're going to be sort of coordinated but not matchy-matchy like we talked about it (even though we have talked about it). Hunter e-mails to ask me if I want to watch him try out for the track team after school. I e-mail back and promise to be there.

The first day is exciting and scary at the same time. Because it's new and old all in one day. New classes, new teachers, new schedules. But also old friends and old routines, like where we meet between classes and for lunch.

For English, I have Mrs. Miller.

"Jane Holden," she calls out from her list.

"Here," I say as I raise my hand.

"Welcome," she greets me. "You are Elizabeth's sister, aren't you?"

"Yes, ma'am," I answer.

"She was my favorite student," Mrs. Miller says with a smile and a warm look in her emerald-colored eyes.

I smile when she tells me. And I remind her that English was Lizzie's favorite subject. I feel happy that someone remembers her and thinks of her so proudly. Mrs. Miller is the only teacher who mentions Lizzie all day.

I have algebra with Zoe and Misty and science with Hunter. Unfortunately, Kirsten Mueller is in my Spanish class. She smirks at me.

At lunch, I sit with Misty and Zoe. We people-watch and talk about our teachers. Hunter walks by with a couple of his friends. He sees me and comes over to say hello. He is shy here at school. But then so am I.

"I'll see you later?" he asks hopefully.

"Definitely," I tell him.

"Cool." He smiles at me.

When he walks away, my friends just stare at me. "What?" I ask, pretending I don't know.

"I guess you are the first one of us to officially have a boyfriend," Zoe announces.

I shrug. "We're just friends." But I can feel my cheeks burning hot.

"Okay," Misty says. "Whatever you say."

I pretend to be nonchalant about the whole thing. But really, inside, I am smiling.

"Did you hear about Kirsten Mueller?" Misty asks after Kirsten and her posse walk past.

"No, what?" I ask, my mouth full of turkey wrap.

"Her parents are splitting up. No one stays together anymore," Misty says.

Poor Kirsten, I think. Instead of thinking that it serves her right for being so horrible to people all the time, I just feel sad about it. I know how I felt when I thought my parents might be getting a divorce. I can only imagine how Kirsten must feel.

"Karma," says Zoe.

Later that day, I am in the girls' bathroom when Kirsten walks in. Alone.

I stare at her.

"What are you looking at, Holden?" she bullies me.

I take a deep breath. I resist the urge to run. I open my mouth and say what I want to say when I want to say it.

"I'm really sorry about your parents," I tell her. "If you ever need someone to listen, let me know."

And then I leave. I don't wait to hear her reply. I don't expect anything from her. But I am proud of myself.

The thing is, from that day forward, Kirsten Mueller stops smirking at me. And every day in Spanish, she says hello to me. We're not going to be best friends, but she's not my enemy anymore either. And that feels good. Causing a change feels good.

Sometimes life has a way of turning things around. So that the things that were upside down are right side up.

On Friday night, Mom and Dad and I watch an old movie together. We share a bowl of buttery popcorn and sit together in the darkened room. We're trying. We're all trying our best to move forward. But it isn't easy. There's always a feeling in the room, of sadness, of uncried tears, and of the longing that you have for someone you will never see again.

After the movie, I stay up late. I close the door to my room and pull out the shoe box from my new sneakers. I get paints, colored paper, markers, and my red-handled scissors. And I start working. On a memory box for Lizzie.

I print out photos of Ethel's roses and decorate the box with flowers. Then I cut out pink hearts, turquoise teardrops, and yellow sunbursts. I glue rhinestones stolen from one of Lizzie's old tutus in the hall closet all over the top of the box.

Inside, I cover the cardboard with a velvet shirt of Lizzie's. I place Lizzie's notebook of poems inside, photos of us as little girls, a copy of *Vogue* magazine. I take her favorite bracelet with a heart charm on it and the number she wore when she ran her first 10k. Her favorite photo of herself. The photo of my mother bringing me home from the hospital. And I place one dried yellow rose from Ethel's garden. Last, I put in the pictures from the funeral.

I cry as I make the box. And I know that it isn't finished. I will add to it over time. But when I close it and slide it underneath my bed, I know that I am ready to help Mom pack up Lizzie's room. I am ready to accept her absence from this world. Because I believe I will see her again. I believe she is with me. And I think she wants me to move forward.

Because loving her and missing her doesn't mean I have to feel sad all the time. And being sorry that she's gone doesn't mean I can't have fun or laugh and smile. It just means that I will always and eternally miss my big sister. And that I will love her forever.

I take the tiny blue box out of the drawer in my bedside table. I look at the silver hoops. I go to the mirror and hold them up. In a few weeks, I can change the piercing earrings for the hoops Lizzie gave me. I can't wait.

I look at myself in the mirror. I look different. Older. Wiser. But I also notice something else.

I am me.

Jane.

And I am perfect. Just the way I am.

ACKNOWLEDGMENTS

Thank you to my agent, Stacey Glick, for your unending faith in me. None of this would have happened without you. Thank you to my editor, Julie Strauss-Gabel, for your guidance and your wisdom—working with you has been an absolute joy. I also want to thank the creative team at Dutton Children's for an exquisite cover, which represents this book so beautifully, and the Dutton Children's Sales and Marketing team for all your work on behalf of this book—I am so grateful. Thank you to my family for your constant love and support and the million things you have done for me. Thank you to my friends for your encouragement and for reading everything I send you. And a special thank you to my daughters, Ava and Caroline—you inspire me every day. I love you.

ays